Oops!

'I' fell in love!

Just by chance ...

Oops!
'I' fell in love!

Just by chance ...

Harsh Snehanshu

Srishti
Publishers & Distributors

Dedicated to all the single girls in this universe. Thanks for providing great relief to the guys.

Srishti Publishers & Distributors
N-16, C. R. Park
New Delhi 110 019
editorial@srishtipublishers.com

First published by
Srishti Publishers & Distributors in 2009

30 29 28 27 26 25

Printed and bound in India

Acknowledgements

Thanking everybody is such an irksome task. But without performing that, any good work remains incomplete. Before you say anything, let me proclaim, *"Yeah, my work is good!"*

Every constructive work needs some fuel as its driving force *(destructive ones need it much more though!)*. The fuel in my case was every little stone of appreciation that I received from my friends all through the way.

So, beginning with the boring task, I first of all thank six of my very special friends – Pallavi, Apoorv, Aman, Ankit, Debanjan and Avinav for proof-reading my whole novel with the most cautious eye I had ever encountered. They had a real fun pulling my leg on each and every blunder that I did. They are so special because I didn't need to think twice before asking them for any favour and moreover, they even forgot to charge any fee from me.

Moving ahead, I genuinely thank another set of my 'awesome' friends – Akshay, Sumi, Supriya, Keshav and Vidhu for being very brutal in pointing out every error in anything I ever wrote; thus giving me a platform to learn, improve and get irritated with them.

I acknowledge my friends for life – Prateek Raj, Ravi, Stuti, Sunny, Kalpana, Jaspreet, Rajiv, Abhinav, Yogesh, Sarvesh, Laveena, Kirtika, Indranuj, Umar, Sagnik, Abhilash, Yash, Aditi, Danvir, Aakanchha and many more for always having faith in my writing and giving me the necessary boost to dream big. I acknowledge all my blogger-pals, since they share the same passion for writing as me and their valuable suggestions did wonders for me.

I am very thankful to the Srishti Publishers and its editorial team for being very professional, prudent and co-operative all throughout the process of publishing.

I can never convey my thanks in words to my sisters-trio Aishwarya, Ayushi and Saumya for being sincere readers-cum-motivators as well as the staunchest critics to my writings. They had a shock of their lifetime reading things, which they could never believe that their so-called *'ideal brother'* had written. They all are still trying to decipher whether this novel is real or fiction. *Keep trying!*

Most important thanks to my Dad and Mom, for endowing me with their genes that could foster extraordinary imagination. Their encouragement towards pursuing my passion with full dedication kept me going in my hard times. *Interestingly, they are yet to be shocked reading my work and realize how well I used their genes!*

Last but not the least, I am thankful to all my girlfriends *(I can't even count the number)* for providing me an insight into the twisted female psychology. *My present girlfriend would kill me after reading this!*

Harsh
Status: Alive
Date: The Eve of 29th August
New Delhi

From Chapter 9

She began thinking about what I had said. Before she could reflect on what I really meant, I averred, "I write – articles…articles, short stories and…and for the past few weeks…I have been planning to write… write a novel."

GOD forgive me for lying! I just wanted to impress her. However, I did have a blog which had been untouched for the past one month. I had written just about a couple of articles in it depicting my miserable condition after getting the grades of my first semester and the hostel politics during the elections. Writing a novel, or even a short story, was a thing that I could not even imagine in my dreams.

"That's impressive. What sort of novel are you planning to write?"

"Umm…A love story" I said without giving prior thought.

It is said that *look before you leap, but once you leap, never look back.* Now since I had leapt, though without even looking, there was no looking back.

"Wow!" She said, her eyes twinkling in curiosity.

"But the only problem is that I don't have any first hand experience of love. I need some experiences which can teach me how it feels to be in love, how separation affects love and what change love brings in a person." I said interrupting her 'wow' midway. Nonetheless, I was back on the road of truth. *Quite relieved.*

A year later, did I realize that she was the one who would give me all the first-hand experiences and would be my inspiration of doing something that I could not have imagined, not even in my dreams.

Part 1

Dilli-ki-hawa

1
The Seductress of the morning!

She was looking at me. Her eyes had desire, a passionate desire. Strikingly beautiful - she was. The soft drizzle rendered her even more beautiful. Lips wet and her clothes drenched kissing her body elucidating her ravishing figure. The curls outlining her face proved to be a slide to the mizzle. My eyes were wide open as if I had just seen God. Actually, I had. Not God, rather a goddess. A goddess, whose flawless beauty was untouched and undiscovered by this world.

Adjectives, I was short of. *Diva-hottie-sexy-ravishing-alluring* were words quite insufficient to describe even a bit of her charm. I was transfixed as if in a trance. I didn't know her and neither did I want to know. But she was with me, I didn't know how! Her presence had captivated me and flushed my mind of all of its *lust-less* thoughts.

Just a meter away from her, I stood. Lost completely, in her ecstatic charm. It was the first time, mine as well as hers.

She stretched her hands; those thin long fingers were going to take me over. Her soft fingers fondled my rain-bathed hair; spoiling my urban hairstyle. It did not matter as long as it was she who was doing so! The fingers didn't stop; they went on and on. Next target, a bit lower was my *bucket-shaped-frustum-like* neck.

The fingers, *nails to be specific*, pricked the slender epidermis of my neck making a drop of fearsome red-fluid trickle down my vertebral column. The rain did a sleek task of diluting the drop of blood making it quite colorless by the time it reached my jeans.

It did hurt; a bit more than a *pinprick*, but the very pain gave pleasure. Immense pleasure. The surrounding was exotic with no trace of life anywhere around us. I held her by her waist. It was just the two of us across the whole globe. Horizon seemed much like *an oil on canvas*, tinges of orange sunlight, which had just set, mixing with the soothing darkness of night.

I pulled her towards me abruptly, my heart waiting for this moment since the day I bawled out on this planet. Our bosoms were kissing each other. *It would be more apt to say that mine was pushing against hers!*

I was going to kiss her – her *wet-pink-n-tempting* lips. I was fully aroused. I just wondered how violent I would be two-minutes later.

I moved closer to her face. I reached her face when her lips took the shape of a circle and she blew her breath at my face. The drizzle that was crossing between our eyes to finally strike our bosoms was sprinkled at my face. I savoured the moment, relished her every mischief and just looked at her. I closed my eyes and moved my lips to seal with hers. It was the moment…the most awaited moment of my life…

"WHO LET THE DOGS OUT
BHOW, BHOW, BHOW-BHOW
WHO LET THE DOGS OUT
BHOW, BHOW, BHOW-BHOW"

This was what struck my ears. *Strange! What was that? I wasn't a singer nor did my face resemble a bulldog.*

This *bhow-bhow-thing* continued to bang my ears with an intermittent tickle near my thighs.

My eyes automatically opened and I could note that she had vanished. How could she? Did she know any magic? *Bhow-bhow-abra-ca-dabra-choo!*

I elevated my line of sight and what I saw was a very familiar face looking intently at me. The face was not quite beautiful, not having even a trace of *her* beauty. The face was, nonetheless, adorned with a *slightly-longer-than-Chaplin* moustache and a *shinier-than-the-moon* top. The eyes were horrendous, being magnified through the *thick-cum-heavy* spectacle that the flattened nose had to carry. Confused, I thought it was an illusion. *Was I still dreaming?* As I analyzed the visual aspect of the face, its auditory aspect exhibited its cruel melody.

"You, get up from your seat." The Thermodynamics Professor asked with his eyes pointing at me in disgust. My nearby sleepers shook me out of my seductive trance.

"Me?" I asked just hoping he had a squint. But, fortunately for him and unfortunately for me, he wasn't. God had given him enough punishment by making him a professor - the most detestable species living on this planet and *'He'* could not be more unjust to him.

"Yes, you..." He censured. His voice stopped at 'you' but his lips didn't. He was flipping through the pages of his lexicon of slangs in his mind which suited students, especially, like me.

"Get out of the class." he thundered.

"Sir, me? But why?"

"You are asking for a why? How dare you sleep in the class?" His voice was increasing its pitch and his blood pressure was shooting up.

My heartbeat was still normal, for a change. I didn't feel nervous, fortunately or unfortunately would be known to me in a while.

"Sir, half of the class sleeps during your lecture. Kick half of them out and then only will I go." I was awed seeing myself so confident for the first time in my three weeks long college-life. It was the seductive dream that stirred all my hormones and sated me with adrenaline to face the first tryst with a professor in my life-time.

I felt no guilt in enlightening my *'dear'* professor of the bitter truth. Half of the sleep-induced audience also joined me and started clapping and banging the desk. The professor showed signs of disgust.

"Shut up. Your mobile too was ringing. Don't argue and just get out of the class." He caught hold of another reason instantly. This time I was on the losing side. But a defeat from a professor was embarrassing. I kept the fighting spirit on, since my stocks of adrenaline were enough to fuel me with confidence.

"No, it wasn't mine. It might be someone else's mobile that was ringing. My mobile is always on silent." I lied with sky-high confidence. I knew the professor had a tough time and he was heading towards defeat.

"This is the last warning I am giving you. Get back to your seat and check your actions otherwise you will be in big trouble."

All hail for Kanav! Oh victory, it tastes so nice!

I turned back in style and as I took my first step towards my seat, a tickle poked my thighs again and the sound

"WHO LET THE DOGS OUT
BHOW, BHOW, BHOW-BHOW
WHO LET THE DOGS OUT
BHOW, BHOW, BHOW-BHOW"

buzzed in all the ears in the class room. That *bhow-bhow* brought an end to my professor's jabbering and all my fellow classmates jested with *all-their-thirty-two-teeth* ready to fall out of their mouths. I could see my roommate Aryan, my hostel-mates Sameer and even Anuj laughing their heads off. Anuj was awake for the first time in the class; his drowsy eyes with a wicked smile did the silent duty of mocking my situation.

I turned my head towards the professor. His eyes had never been so frenzied. He was a step short of strangling my throat with the barbed wires circumscribing the institute's campus. Just at the moment the professor opened his mouth to explode on me, I rushed out of the room making the swiftest exit possible.

As soon as I left the room, the ringtone of my cell-phone stopped buzzing and left me startled of its perfect timing. I took out the cell-phone just to realize that it was my room-mate Aryan and the gang who had spoilt my ravishing dream and even ruined my chances of defeating the professor.

This was not the first time when I slept while a lecture was on, but this was the first time when I forgot to put my cell on silent. And my 'loyal' friends left no stone unturned to provide themselves some entertainment amidst the deadening thermodynamics scattered all over the black-board.

I was reflecting upon what I had done. Instead of being worried, I was surprised to see myself bubbling with confidence. *Was it because of the dream?* The 'She' in the dream had given a sudden hike in my self-esteem. I was feeling proud of myself for the first time!

I stood beside the window staring blankly at the overwhelming panorama of the majestic architecture of the Dogra-hall - the auditorium of IIT- Delhi. Thoughts started flooding my mind, the thoughts with the elements of question, pride and remorse veiled in them.

Something had happened!

That was one of those yet another days of my newly-begun college life. Before I move any further, let me introduce myself - Hi, I am Kanav Bajaj. *Cool name, isn't it?*

Life has really changed for me after coming to Delhi, a city of dreams. It had been just three weeks since I am here and I could observe some drastic changes in me. A simple lad from Indore has become a totally outrageous guy in this city. Two years of frying my bottom and hammering my head with all kinds of test papers has landed me in IIT and made me different from the rest of the world - an unparalleled species for the general *janta* around us.

IIT is one of the most uniquely endowed places of the world. Endowed in three great respects, with the species called the *professors, girls and geeks* – IIT is an unparalleled *khichdi* of three of the most unique phyla of the world. It seems as if God was doing a '*pick and choose*' and he sent all the unwanted creatures to a special prison cell called IIT: *Institute for Insipid Tortures.*

Professors are stale*(you are the exception, if you happen to be my professor).* Their faces seem as if they have just survived a cannibal-attack. Baldness is a prerequisite for their selection in the faculty, with even very young professors getting a *shining-moon-on-their-head.*

From class 10th, I had been hammered about IIT. And after achieving it, I am roving around – goal-less. A sudden change of environment has resulted in lack of ambition within me. I am a lonely wanderer having no idea where I am heading to.

Contrary to your perception, the IITians are not the luckiest chaps around the nation, in fact, their problem is very poignant and complex. Talking about the main IIT population which means guys – a hell lot of guys*(leaving the gays and 'non-guys' lot!)* – the scrimpy sex-ratio leaves no stone unturned to make you realize that you did a heinous crime by having your orientation straight. You have got only two choices - either make a girlfriend in the first year itself or be a celibate for the next four years. *Four years? Isn't it too much!*

Unfortunately, there are very few good-looking girls with the tag 'TO LET'; once they cross a one-year mark in Delhi.

By the end of the first year, the guys who took the vow of celibacy end up being *despo* i.e. *guys with their hunting-mode always on.* The medley of all kinds of students from all kinds of background gives IIT a special place. The first semester takes it toll on these guys and it secretly activates the *despo-genome* in them. The geeky eyes start seeking pleasure, of all kinds, and the inter-hostel LAN connection helps easy transmission of the pleasurable-objects. Interestingly, this *despo* tag is much more popular than the IIT-tag.

Had the Delhi University been closer to the IIT then the bunch of *proud-to-be-an-IITian-stuff* might have been able to satiate their emotional needs. The emotional needs are surprisingly too many to pen down. The continuous tryst with the sadistic professors, the number of girls being zilch and the unconquerable *peer* pressure are just a few specks of harassment, to mention here.

The peers consist of *talented-but-vella-guys* in bulk who follow the pop-ideology of *chill-maaro* with an exemplary zeal and a miniscule amount of geeks and nerds with dishevelled hair and stinky trousers, who seem like they haven't bathed for the past two years for the sake of their FIITJEE assignments.

It's another thing that the *chill-maar-type-guys* look geekier than the nerds during the exams courtesy their struggle to assimilate the whole book in a single night-out.

Talking about my yesteryears, the years that shaped my *irksome* adolescence, I was quite naive and simple. Regarding girls, I was simpler. I was quite unacquainted and untouched by their *mind-baffling-seductively-wow-qualities*, being submerged in the stagnant ocean of preparation for the JEE.

However, my entry in the capital of the nation has had its effect on me naturally - in short - I could not find myself *a perfect wind-cheater* to protect myself from this *dilli-ki-hawa!* It had its effect on me and still I am under its spell, though with no achievements. No achievements – perhaps due to how I look or something else.

How do I look? I know that is the obvious question knocking your mind. So here is the answer.

My appearance is not next to Brad Pitt or the contemporaries. Considering Delhi, I am by far one of the middle 25%-50% in terms of the guys and gays of Delhi with respect to the looks.

I am nevertheless fair, thanks to my parents but I have a very average-height 5'9", no-thanks to my parents this time. I have spectacles giving me a look of a geek, but that doesn't affect me as it is the unsaid trademark of being intelligent. Without the spectacles I look really good, but no-one looks good to me – that's the myopia-tragedy – anyone who is standing at a distance of more than a meter looks hazy much as those censored-pics of Iraq prisoners-of-war.

Then there are *braces* making my face look a bit better than Goofy and recently I got those pimples that make the constellation *Orion* on my left cheek and the *Big Dipper* on the other.

So this is me. *And yeah, I am single.*

"Who let the dogs out…
Who let the dogs out…"

The tone buzzed in my ears, yet again. This time it was not my cell phone that spoke up. Rather, it was the chorus of my classmates whose singing could really make anyone think – *'Who let the dogs out?'*

I was brought back to the present. The majestic view captivated my eyes, once again and I could see my reflection in the window pane, my braces scintillating in the sunshine.

"Enjoyed your tryst with Thermodynamics?" Anuj tapped me from behind. He was smiling. Sameer followed. Classes got over, quite soon.

"Certainly. Damn you all." I said, with my voice clearly showing my disgust.

"Man, what gave you so much courage?" Anuj asked.

"I was confused. Being shaken directly from the dream state, what else do you expect?" I said irritably.

"Dream? What kinda' dream?"

"It was a splendid dream. I was about to kiss a beauty when…" I said.

"Your *bhow-bhow* started." Anuj said and laughed, rather neighed like a horse. Sameer too was enjoying a chuckle providing a distorted background music.

"We were shocked to see you in that mode! Even Prof was faltering in front of you." Sameer said.

"I thought I was still dreaming…and tried to become a hero in that dream!" I said repugnantly.

"Hero, sure! The professor will definitely make a hero out of you." Anuj said sarcastically.

"Did the professor say anything afterwards?" I asked.

"The Professor said - 'These kind of guys bring a bad name to IIT. IIT is not an end, but a beginning. You got to work hard if you want to succeed at the world level. Little things make perfection but perfection in itself is not a little thing.' He also said…" Sameer said and his 24/7 broadcast was still on.

"Shut up dog! I don't want to hear all that crap! Keep your mouth shut." I said and interrupted his exaggerated version of Professor's lecture.

"He just noted your name, I don't know why." Anuj said while I changed back the *bhow-bhow* ringtone of my mobile to the sober Nokia tune.

"Hey I got to go. Have some important work to do. See you guys later." Anuj said eyeing Neetika, one of the few girls IIT possessed, who was just passing by. We bid him a slight wave on his sacred task of flirting with the fairer sex.

"By the way, where is that bloody Aryan?" I asked.

"I don't know. Must be hiding from you." Sameer chuckled.

"Bloody pig!" I said.

2
The PIG and Other Domestic Animals!

Once upon a time, three weeks ago...

"Hi, are you Kanav?" A handsome guy was standing at the door wearing a low-waist so low that just one jump could strip him off. Everything constituting his attire was branded, even his underwear since I could see a strap of '*the next best thing to naked*' popping its head out of his jeans. Soon, followed his driver who looked more like a porter with three heavy bags on his shoulder and a bedding rolled up on his head.

This Adonis is going to be my room-mate. I would not even dare to look at myself in the mirror in front of him.

"Yeah, you are Aryan, I suppose." I said in a voice with concealed enthusiasm.

For a *moustache-till-plus-two* kind of guy like me, a room-mate with Hollywood looks and metrosexual-style was nothing less than a permanent source of inferiority complex.

"Hi, room-mate! How are you? When did you reach?"

"Hi. I am doing great. I reached at 8 in the morning. Why are you so late?"

"Oh me, I got up late." He said with such an ease as if the first day in IIT was just another day in his life.

He emptied his bags. Other than few more imported garments plus undergarments and perfumes, he had every other thing in triples. Three perfumes, three pairs of shoes, a triad of goggles and what-not. Strange, it seemed to me.

"What's with this number three? All your things happen to be in triads?"

"It's a kind of lucky number for me. My birthday is on 3rd March and so the number three is quite close to me. Even my All India Rank was 333. What was yours by the way?"

"Oh mine was 993, quite far from yours, still being related to your 3 in some way or the other." I was perplexed seeing such an urban guy following some illogical bullshit.

"Oh fuck, fuck, fuck! I forgot to bring my laptop." Aryan said in his quite natural tone as he could not find his laptop bag in the room. It was the first time I heard the 'F' word out of somebody's mouth, that too not once or twice but *thrice*. I preferred using an 'Oops' instead of that most commonly used word in Delhi, until the next two weeks of exposure to hundreds of such triads had a transforming effect on me.

"Don't seniors rag those who bring laptops and smart gadgets, the first time?"

"Oh seniors, let them come. Bloody fuckers will have the time of their life. I have brought great entertainment for them." He said pointing to a twenty gigabytes pen-drive which, as he said, carried enough eye-pleasing work to give the seniors *the time of their life*.

Aryan dumped all the things in the most haphazard manner on the table, chairs and the racks. His bed offered no space for him to sit and he came to my side and took one of my chairs for the time being.

"There is a cupboard over there where you can put these things." I said pointing to the *two-peach-colored-doors* hanging on the wall with the help of *three* hinges.

"Oh yeah but that's for old and used dirty clothes." He said smiling at me.

He was weird. His newly occupied room looked as if it had been not arranged for the past two weeks. All the gizmos were scattered around.

"Any girlfriends?" Aryan asked all of a sudden.

"Oh me, no. What about you?" I followed my reflex.

"Just had an official break-up – for the second time in my life. Right now, looking for a hot chick. She would be the third – the luckiest one" Aryan said. I was awed hearing the ease with which he said that he had a break-up. He did not look sad at all. All the same, his experience sparked jealousy in me.

I always believed that love is forever but seeing no guilt on Aryan's face made me feel strange. For Aryan, love indeed was forever, it was just that for him, the word 'forever' meant two months at max.

Meanwhile, Aryan emptied his bag of gizmos. I began counting the number of gadgets he possessed, when a bizarre wail struck both of our ears.

"Someone is sobbing. The sound seems to be coming from the next room." I said.

We proceeded in the direction of the sound. It was coming from the room next to us. As we entered the room, we observed that a guy was sitting on his bed and crying. His room-mate was yet to arrive.

"What happened buddy? Is everything fine?" Aryan asked. We proceeded and stood in front of him. His room was arranged perfectly, with a simple bed-sheet on his bed and no objects showcasing even a pinch of extravagance.

"My parents left for Bhubhaneshwar. It is the first time I am away from them. I am missing them." He replied and pulled back the *ready-to-fall* fluids up his nose in one go.

He was thin; his ribs seemed to bestow his body with an eight-pack abs, and had a kind of cute face. He looked much as a grade-10 child, with *yet-to-be-bearded* face and a trifle hint of a moustache. I was just a mute spectator to his sorrows, busy decoding his looks more than his pains. He was much like me, from a relatively small-town and a middle-class family but still he was completely different by being a typical Mama's boy. My parents too left for Indore, my hometown, but I was not homesick at all. I was kind of relishing this newly-found independence with no restrictions yet mysterious responsibilities.

"You are such a kiddo! Wait let me bring something for you, you will relish it." Aryan exclaimed irritably.

"What?" The homesick said looking curiously. I was also curious seeing Aryan behaving creepy.

Aryan went back to our room while I stayed. Though the sob stopped, the tears were still on. I was about to say something, when he spoke.

"Hey have a seat." He said pointing to the chair.

"Thanks. I am Kanav, and you are?" I asked extending my right hand in greeting.

"I am Anuj. What's that smart guy's name?" Anuj asked. I was astonished to note that Aryan's persona attracted even guys' attention.

"Aryan. He is my room-mate."

"I got something for you." Aryan was back with two colourful magazines in his hand.

In just the next two seconds, new words like Debonair and Maxim were introduced into my vocabulary. It was the first time that I noticed that beauty was much more than just the face. *Much much more.* Seeing the enticing cover, Anuj's face lightened up with a million-dollar smile as if the model on the cover was his lost girlfriend. With eyes wide open, he relished every bit of the ongoing experience. In no time, his home became a memory of past and his stock of tears mutated into *something else* down his body.

"See him. Bloody astute! See the smile that he has while missing his parents." Aryan said to me.

"His eyes are going to pop outside his skull." I said even though my eyes were nearly in the same position, if not more.

I was feeling a bit strange by what suddenly happened. I was in a state of fear, experiencing an inherent disability to take pleasure in so-called immensely delightful moments. I took the magazine and moved towards the next bed, which was unoccupied since Anuj's roommate was yet to arrive.

My room-mate initiated us into the erotica on the very first day of my college. A two minutes long date with the magazine was more than enough to sublimate my anhedonia. My eyes lost their virginity. Both of us were busy flipping through the pages of the *bold-yet-beautiful* and it brought a joy never experienced before. Being brought up in an environment when an 'A' sign before a movie meant I was not going to watch it, this sudden change sparked *a sinful pleasure* in my mind. All my conscience and the so-called *sanskaras* dissolved in the universal solvent of lust.

Without a knock, the door of Anuj's room squeaked. A guy carrying a big mattress and two heavy-roller bags entered the room. Chubby, with a slight paunch protruding in the front and big-bums doing the same at the back, he seemed to be over-laden with the luggage plus his own weight. His sunken eyes clearly hinted that he had been sleep-deprived for the last two years.

We, all at once, stood up to help him out.

"Hey guys, I am Sameer."

"Hi." We all replied in unison.

"Hey what's that? A porno magazine! What is it doing on my bed?" Sameer said with frenzied look in his eyes.

"I was just flipping through it." I said blushingly.

"Wanna have a look. See page number 75, it will blow your mind." Aryan said with a *know-it-all* attitude on his face.

"Shut up! You shitty fellows! You don't respect the dignity of women. How cheap! We are an educated bunch of guys and if we do such heinous acts then what example are we going to set for others?" That was just Sameer's beginning. It marked the commencement of his never-ending ideologies and philosophies which had enough power to even confuse Aristotle.

"Are you ok? It's such a trivial matter." Anuj asked.

"It is not. Guys go and have some fresh air to let go of your lust." Sameer ordered and we all followed.

"He is a psycho! I wonder what would be my condition with him for the entire semester." Anuj complained after all of us got a discomfiting look from his room-mate. Aryan also lost his serenity after that debacle. We three were standing at the balcony having a grand view of the swimming pool as well as the road in front of us.

"Whatever, just don't become like him. He is an idealist. Must have been Gandhi in his previous incarnation." I joked which no-one appreciated.

"Bloody heck! What does this guy think of himself? These kind of guys should be ragged so severely that all their philosophies are flushed out." Aryan said. He was angry, perhaps because Sameer did not open the page he asked him to.

There were some girls passing by the road, seemed like the *fachchis* were getting acquainted with the campus.

"C'mon guys. I have something to please your mind." Aryan exclaimed out of the blue.

"Now, what else?" I exclaimed irritably considering how his last *please-your-mind* thing was received.

"C'mon!" Aryan exclaimed.

The pleasing thing turned out to be the brand-new *fachchis – the rare combination of plumpness with brains*, who were to be our company for the next four years. Aryan had some of the female-friends during coaching for JEE who *accidentally* cracked it. My city nevertheless boasted of me as the topper out of only a few guys who made it to the IIT.

Considering the crappy encounters with Sameer, we hoped to find something more interesting than him. Aryan, Anuj and I jumped over the stairs at a great pace just to have that pleasurable glimpse of the other sex.

"Hey Swati." Aryan called from behind to a group of three ladies who were busy in the inspection of the campus.

"Hieee, Aryan. Which hostel have you got?" Swati reciprocated in surprise. She was a bit chubby but nevertheless cute. She was surrounded by two more girls, looking much like new entrants with sunken eyes, spectacles and a slight paunch. Their arms had more muscles than Anuj had. All their eyes were resting upon Aryan - in surprise or awe, I don't know!

"I got Zanskar. What about you?" Aryan asked.

"Himadri, the best amongst the two!" Swati replied with pride.

How worthy is it to be the best amongst two?

Anuj was busy analyzing Swati and her mates from top to bottom. It seemed that he was still under the spell of the debonair-effect. I coughed, just to disturb Anuj's concentration spell.

"Oh! I forgot to introduce you all to my friends. He is Kanav – my roommate and this is Anuj." Aryan said. My coughing perhaps caught Aryan's attention. I waved a 'hi' and just smiled, being conscious not to show my braces.

"Anuj…hmm." Swati just repeated Anuj's name. His ridiculous action during the first meet was enough to make his name enter their brain forever.

"Hi girls." Anuj flirted.

"They are my hostel-mates – Neetika and Reva." The names got imprinted on my memory.

"Ok, you are the same guy who added me on Orkut. Anuj Roy – Zanskar Hostel." Neetika asked Anuj and all the other girls had their gestures anticipating Anuj's introduction.

"Yeah. I think I know all of you. Neetika Sharma, Swati Khandelwal and Reva Chaudhary – Himadri house. Isn't it?" Anuj said. He had befriended almost every girl going to join the institute beforehand through Orkut.

"Yeaaa…ah!!!" They exclaimed with a joy as if they had found their lost brother in him.

Anuj became quite involved in the conversation, Aryan was already involved and I was playing the role of a shrub in the background busy in discerning whether God had gifted me with a tongue or not. I just could not muster up the courage to speak anything. I was staring at them – with an infinite blankness painting my face.

"You can also join the talk." Reva said to me and all of them laughed. I could not find anything funny in her statement, but I was embarrassed.

"Oh yeah, sure." I said very consciously. My scalp was converted into a combustion engine and my heartbeat climbed several notches upwards. Without even having any locks of hair, I was transformed into Shiva with the *Ganges of sweat* trickling down my head from all the four sides.

My phone rang and I got a life-saving excuse to save myself from being labeled as *fattu* in front of them. Their talks continued and finally ended with the exchange of phone numbers. I did not say a word in the whole conversation other than my *oh-yeah-sure.*

The guys returned to me while I was still busy listening to all kinds of tender suggestions which a Mom could pour on her child who was away from home for the first time in his entire life.

"I am going Ma, my friends are coming. Bye." I ended my conversation.

" 'Mr. *Oh yeah sure.*' Wazzup?" Anuj said.

"What's the use of having a phone when you know just one thing and that is nodding your head?" Aryan mocked my gynophobia. They continued the severe mockery of my behavior for sometime. After gifting me a bucket full of ridicule their topic shifted to who amongst them was the best, thus providing me a great relief. It is really a tough task to compare between equal competitors with almost the same features.

"I really liked Neetika. She is good-looking." Anuj said.

"Man, this is Delhi. You could find numerous better than her."

Aryan rebuked. He was really uninfluenced by any of them, though half the time their eyes rested upon him.

"Oh really. I will see." Anuj said. I wondered what he meant by '*I-will-see*'.

"Which one did you like Kanav? Rather which one made you *wet?*" Aryan said. They both jested at the double-meaning pun that Aryan used. I had no comments to make.

"Leave him. His tongue must be parched; after all, he spoke so much in front of them…to his Mom, of course." Anuj said sarcastically followed by a growling giggle.

"Will you please give me a break. Don't you have any other topic to roast your brain with?" I shouted after I felt that they had crossed their limit.

"Back to where we belong – the proud Zanskarites!" Anuj exclaimed and maturely shifted the topic of discussion.

"Back to the crap – your room. That weirdo is gonna chew your brains out!" Aryan said with his voice giving a clear hint of his annoyance at Sameer. Anuj pushed the door but it was locked from inside.

"Hey don't knock. If he is sleeping, then he might get angry." I said considering the short tempered attitude Sameer showered upon all of us some minutes ago.

"You are right. Let us see what that creep is doing and then accordingly we will knock. Kanav, form a horse!" Anuj ordered.

"A horse?"

"Yeah, bend down so that we can see through the ventilators what that scoundrel is up to!" Aryan said. Every sentence that his tongue fabricated was ornamented with a special word just to impart some personal touch.

I bent down and branch-like thin Anuj stood on my back. He could not reach the ventilators.

"Move, let me climb up on Kanav." Aryan whispered and climbed on my back. My backbone had to give a test of endurance. A six-feet tall guy was on my back with his entire weight distributed on my four limbs.

"Bloody hell, that guy is glued to my magazines!" Aryan exclaimed.

Aryan jumped off my back and I heaved a sigh of relief. The backbone-test lasted for about 10 seconds and I emerged out alive. Anuj clamped his fist hard on the door. The door shuddered under the impact. We were in shock.

Sameer jumped to the door in an instant, came forward with a smile and said over-pleasantly, "You people returned quite early!"

The smile on his face was not genuine enough to hide his agitation. We didn't speak a word.

"What's the matter? Why is everyone staring at me?" Sameer interrogated.

"Oh wow. How did these magazines travel from Anuj's bed to yours'? Did you teach them how to walk?" I asked sarcastically. Seeing somebody, other than me, being tortured, in no time did I discover my lost tongue.

"Oh, these…umm…oops!" Sameer was out of words and full of sweat.

"Bloody hypocrite! Damn you. Scoundrel!" Aryan was doing the thing he was best at. His tongue was really gifted.

Two minutes later, Sameer's heavy ass got roasted with a perfect thrashing. Other new entrants too joined us to make the show quite successful. I could observe a sadistic smile on all our faces; and even Sameer had a smile – but a vertical one though.

I made space through the crowd to have my take on Sameer with my pointed canvas shoe. I lifted my right leg and leaned back to provide me some balance while striking the target. Anuj caught my right hand and lifted me and the whole crowd dropped Sameer down and exercised their football-skills on me. Huh. This was not fair. Aryan shouted, "Don't be merciful guys; he has no balls…just carry on."

I knew why he said that and I know that he was not wrong, not literally though. I was disgusted. I felt a sudden repulsion against all of them. But that's how college life was! Days on, the mischief went on, with targets for attack being shifted from me to Sameer to Anuj. Aryan was still untouched, though.

A string of similar disasters in the past three weeks bombed my self-confidence and frequent sweaty encounters with the other sex, because of hanging around with Aryan, sky-rocketed my misery. Though now, after three weeks, I had learnt quite a lot of stuff, but I still had a lot of work to do. I still lacked the balls to make my tongue work in front of any girl.

3
A Bucket of Proposals

"I love Neetika." Anuj whispered to Aryan. I overheard them talking, not quite intentionally though.

"Neetika? How could you? Just three weeks made you fall in love with her." Aryan stated in shock. I stood up and went on to join the conversation. Anuj hesitated to speak ahead.

"I know her very well. I have talked with her for hours on net and even personally I could feel that she likes me." Anuj said.

"What's the urgency?" I said, appearing all of a sudden in the conversation.

"Some seniors told me that if you want to make an IIT girl your girlfriend, then the initial few weeks are the perfect time. And Neetika is definitely the best one of the lot." Anuj said. His immaturity made me feel disgusted.

"Duffer, seniors brainwashed you. As far as I think, gaining trust is the first step in any relationship. First you need to be a best friend to finally become the mate." I poured down all my *middle-class-perception* of love, which indeed was very true.

"Stop being Sameer. Keep your bull-shit philosophies to yourself. If you know so much, then why can't you utter a single word in front of the girls?" Aryan reprimanded.

I could not utter a single word in reply to his rebuke. Though they were not girls – not even a slice of feminine character could I find in them, but still I was mute.

"I want help, Aryan. If you can then do, otherwise get lost." Anuj said.

"Say! I am ready." Aryan said. His temper was brought back to the ground level.

"Can you please ask Swati and her friends for a get-together at some place. I know that I won't be able to fix up a date with Neetika, no matter how much I try. But I also know that they won't deny you. Swati likes you, you know that! Tell them it's my birthday party." Anuj exploited Aryan's popularity amongst girls to the best.

"Ok." Aryan said.

"Swati likes Aryan? How do you know?" I asked in shock. I didn't know this much.

"Haven't you seen her Orkut profile? Her ideal match's description is totally similar to Aryan's personality." Anuj flaunted his Orkut expertise. After all, his ten thousand scraps on Orkut was not a small accomplishment.

Aryan fixed up a gathering on 23rd August, 2007 for Anuj's imaginary birthday at the Ansal's Plaza. For a change, to accompany those three girls, Sameer and I proved to be the appropriate company.

At Ansal's Pizza Hut, a table of seven and just an hour of wait, already!

Anuj had never looked so handsome before. His petite body complemented his funky T-shirt saying "*If only you knew*". He was nevertheless quite nervous. Anuj got a wrapped empty gift-box as a gift from all three of us. We all waited for the girls – for *just one hour.*

"If they don't come now, then I am gonna jump off this building." Anuj said.

"I am asking them not to come. Neetika's life will be saved for sure." Aryan ridiculed.

"Suicide is the permanent solution to any temporary problem. Go for it roommate. I will get a ten pointer by default if you do so." Sameer taunted Anuj. His funny statements too contained a bit of philosophy.

"Here they come." I said as soon as I saw the group of *plump-beauties* coming towards us. Anuj began to comb his hair with his sleek fingers. Sameer too pulled his paunch in and smiled at them.

"Hi girls!" Aryan exclaimed and the bunch reciprocated.

"Happy birthday Anuj. You never told me that you were a Virgo. Virgos and Scorpions make great friends." Reva said.

I felt repulsive. I was allergic to horoscopes, clairvoyance and all those stuff. I observed Reva's face carefully and for a moment I was bemused since she looked like a tarot card reader with lots of kajal lining her eyelids.

"Happy birthday." Neetika said and shook hands with Anuj. It was perhaps their first touch.

"Thanks. That's great." Anuj said as he accepted the gift from Neetika's hands.

Neetika got a call and she went on phone.

Meanwhile, Aryan asked all three of us to come near him. The girls were too busy chattering amongst themselves to take notice of our secret plan in execution.

"Listen, Kanav and I are moving around. In the mean time Sameer, you take those two girls with you to get the birthday cake and leave Neetika aside. And when she gets free from the phone, she is all yours gentleman! Go and flush out your feelings for her." He said to Anuj with a smile.

Anuj was visibly anxious and he got his sweat-glands active in the air-conditioned ambience of the mall. With a slight 'huh', Anuj shook hands and we wished him luck. Sameer went towards the gang of girls while we headed the other way, upstairs.

"I need to use the loo." I said to Aryan.

"My bladder also needs relaxation. Let's go upstairs." Aryan said.

It took us at least half a dozen escalators to finally find a place to shed the excess liquid. Aryan entered the washroom whistling the tune of "*Bheege hont tere*" and went towards the side-most cubicle. I went exactly to the other side as I preferred some solitude while doing my private job. Meanwhile a strange guy entered the washroom, he kept moving here and there for sometime and then he straightaway went to Aryan's adjacent cubicle, smiling at both of us. His lips were abnormally pink and he had a strange tattoo peeping out of the base of his neck.

He tried to peek into Aryan's cubicle when Aryan suddenly retreated. I had also finished my task and we went back to the wash basin.

"He is drunk. He smelled like shit." Aryan whispered in my ears.

"What was he doing with you?"

"He is a homo let's get away from here." Aryan said hurriedly.

The strange guy followed.

"Hey Duke, where had you been? I had spent so many nights without you. I missed you a lot." The guy literally jumped on Aryan. He smelt of alcohol.

Meanwhile, Neetika finished her call. She moved back to find that no-one other than the gentleman-in-action a.k.a Anuj was present.

"Where have the others gone?" Neetika asked Anuj.

"They didn't tell me about it. Might be for cake or something." Anuj said.

Neetika looked around the corridor and then back at Anuj. His eyes were already lost in adoring her. Her eyes rolled down to his T-shirt and she stared at it for long. Anuj realized that this was the moment which could define his entire life. He bent down on one of his haunches as if he were to tie his shoe laces. Neetika thought the same and her eyes drifted around when suddenly her hand felt a soft touch - the touch of a red rose. Anuj was proposing to her.

"The day I first saw you, I went crazy. It has been only you and you who haunted...oops...appeared in my dreams. I just want to say that I love you."

Neetika was overwhelmed and was still in shock. Her eyes were staring blankly at Anuj and her hand could not move at all to get hold of the rose he offered.

Taking deep breaths in, she said, "I really appreciate your feelings for me, but I don't have the same feelings for you. I am really very sorry. I don't want to hurt you. You have always been my friend but I can't say a 'yes'."

"But why? Tell me why?" Anuj cried in despair.

---

500 bucks down, Sameer was cursing Aryan for assigning him with the work of getting the cake. Though, he got some listeners of his *different* style of thinking, he still was not happy.

"I always love birthdays. It brings people close to each other, the warmth and harmony increases. It gives you the opportunity to make others feel special. Make me feel special by contributing 100 bucks each! Just kidding!" Sameer said. They were having their first dose of Sameer. Instead of being amused, they turned bemused with his weird sense of humour.

Swati was lost in her own thoughts being totally indifferent to Sameer's bull-shit while Reva found Sameer her type, in short, a chatterbox.

"This chocolate one is nice. I just love chocolates." Reva said pointing to the cake.

"Me too." Sameer echoed and smiled.

"What gift had you brought for Anuj?" Sameer asked.

"A deodorant. Could not find anything better." Reva said.

"Deo? Does he stink?" Sameer asked, making them laugh. His every sentence did a sleek task of incrementing Swati's irritation.

"You better know, after-all you are his room-mate." Swati said in a snobbish tone.

"Whatever, the end result is my room is gonna be fragrant. I am happy." Sameer said.

"What gift have you bought?" Reva asked.

"Oh we… we…umm… bought a set of pens…and a card… and a key ring too. Yeah, that's all. That's all." Sameer faltered all the way.

"I am getting a headache. I am going back to sit somewhere. You people get the cake and come back." Swati said and detached herself from the company of two chatterboxes. She strolled around and went back to the same place where she had left Neetika.

Aryan pushed him aside and shouted, "Run!" to me.

The guy followed us.

"I don't understand why that scoundrel is following me. Who is this Duke? Why is he referring to me as Duke?" Aryan shouted while running to save his life.

We romped down the steps of the escalators and did not dare to look back. In haste, we stepped on an ascending escalator and rolled down the way. And in no time, the two glasses of my spectacle became seven. With bruised elbows and gasping breaths, we kept rushing towards our other friends. All through the way, only one thought struck my mind: *GAYS DO EXIST!*

Out of breath and a bit relieved finding that 'Duke's lover' was out of sight, we took a break and sat down on the bench lying on the way.

"Where were you running? Let me see what have you stolen bloody crooks!" A tall muscular guard was standing in front of us with a lathi in his hand.

"But why? Tell me why?" Anuj cried in despair.

"Because I love Aryan." She said loudly and two huge drops of tears rolled down her cheeks.

Anuj felt choked, as if somebody had put a vacuum cleaner in his mouth and sucked whole of the saliva out of his tongue. His hands were now holding his head and the red rose had become a part of the floor. Neetika turned to the other side and tried to impose discipline on her tear glands.

Moments passed. Neetika felt uncomfortable in his company. She moved away from him, in search of the rest of the group.

"Because I love Aryan." Swati overheard Neetika's last statement. She reached behind her just at the time when she said that. It pierced through her heart.

She could not resist somebody eyeing her heart-throb since her coaching days. Though she had never conveyed this to Aryan, thinking she was too unattractive to complement him but she did not want to lose him to anyone – in this case this 'anyone' was just her month-long friend Neetika.

Without wasting a moment, she followed her way back and began looking for Aryan.

"Trying to escape? You can't escape the security of this mall. Hands up! Let me check what you have stolen bloody bastards!" A tall muscular guard was standing in front of us with a *lathi* in his hand. He could not find anything spectacular out of our pockets. On-lookers stared at us making us feel like petty thieves.

"Sir, there was one guy who was …following…us and we… were running away from him and had a terrible fall." I said with pauses to catch my breath.

"We are just students. There was somebody drunk who was following us; we were just running away from him. We can show you our I-cards, if you wish." Aryan stated.

"C'mon show me your I-cards." The guard asked us.

He left us after analyzing every bit of the face on each of the I-cards with ours. He would have been disappointed finding our face not resembling any of the terrorists; after all no famous terrorist had got braces decorating his face or was visibly handsome.

I turned my head around to find a place for water when I saw that tattooed guy again. The guard had disappeared then and we had no option left other than to run again.

"Hey Aryan, that guy is coming this way. Let us hide. Shit, he has seen us." I said.

"That fucker is smiling at me." Aryan said.

We moved faster, this time we did not run as we thought of catching him and calling the security.

"Aryan!" A shriek bombed my ears. Swati was running towards Aryan across the corridor. Aryan stood there perplexed and waited for her. Swati came near him and at the same time *Mr. Tattoo* also stepped into his proximity.

"I love you." Swati said to Aryan.

Aryan was dumbfounded. His legs could not move for a while and his eyes were fixed on Swati's. I was literally paralyzed seeing what happened so suddenly. Swati moved ahead and embraced Aryan tightly.

"Hey Anuj, where is Neetika? Why are you alone?" Sameer asked. He and Reva were back with the chocolate cake.

Anuj wiped his tears and with an imposed smile on his face replied, "Don't know. She would be somewhere here only."

Sameer wiggled his eyebrows to enquire Anuj about the proposal without saying a word. Anuj negated by shaking his head.

"What happened?" Sameer asked. Meanwhile, Reva began arranging the cake on the table.

"Hey Anuj, please open this gift." Reva said giving Anuj the empty wrapped box.

"Today is not my birthday. And that box is empty. I am sorry I lied to you all." Anuj said.

"What? What for?" Reva asked.

"I wanted to propose to Neetika and ..." Anuj broke into tears.

"Damn you! At least you should have told us about it. Is this a time to propose...you hardly had a talk with her..." Reva snapped from the two guys and went in search of the other girls. Sameer sympathized with Anuj but Anuj was heart-broken.

Aryan saw that guy coming towards him and just to make him realize that he was straight, he took a bizarre step. Though he had no special feelings for Swati, he reciprocated Swati's '*I love you*' with an embrace.

"Aryan, you love Swati? Then why had you been giving me looks during the classes?" A shrill voice drilled into my ears. It was Neetika, she appeared out of nowhere. She could not withstand the ongoing public display of affection. I was shocked. *What happened to Anuj? Does Neetika like Aryan? Could Anuj propose to Neetika?*

"I don't love her and neither you..." Aryan surrendered to the situation. Swati looked at Aryan's face, appalled. Neetika was devastated.

"That's because he loves me!" The guy spoke breaking the ghastly lull. The rosy-lipped guy just reached our place and stood by my side. He heard Aryan's last statement.

"Don't you remember that night Duke? You were so hard that night. We had an awesome time together." The guy said.

Hearing this, Neetika lost herself and she fainted when I caught hold of her. It was the first time my hands had encountered any girl. I was just feeling lucky. Though my broken spectacles could not offer much clarity of vision but my hands could feel her body-temperature. I could hear her breaths.

Utterly shocked with what the guy said, Swati kicked Aryan's most vulnerable part, while they were still hugging. She freed herself from him and went away in a huff. Aryan suffered harshly, without any reason. Meanwhile, Reva came and was stunned seeing the hapless situation. Aryan was groaning in pain and the tattooed guy offering him help – *all kinds of help,* and I was holding fainted Neetika in my hands.

Reva came towards me and slapped me hard. It was the first time any girl touched my cheeks but alas, the touch shook even my jaws.

"What are you doing with her?" Reva said to me.

"Bring some water. She has fainted." I said. A small crowd gathered around us.

"You go and bring water. Leave her now!" Reva rebuked.

I came back with a bottle of water and fortunately Neetika had regained her consciousness by then. They gathered themselves and went away.

I heard Reva saying to Neetika, "Do you know it wasn't Anuj's birthday. They are bloody liars."

Aryan stood up after recovering from the pain and lost his temper. The fire of revenge whirled in his mind and he caught that guy's collar. He kicked hard in between the guy's legs, and allowed him to see stars on the ground. He never would have experienced such a *high* in his alcoholic life.

The girls were no longer around us. It was just the four of us – the Fantastic Four with the chocolate cake in front of us.

Sameer ate the chocolate cake with a little bit of help from me. Though Sameer cursed each one of us for making his heavy wallet empty, he relished the cake, after-all it proved to be nourishment for sustaining his paunch. He was quite unaffected with whatever happened. He had just two things that were enough to keep him occupied his whole life – chewing sweets and chewing brains.

Minutes later we too went back to the hostel, after-all we were like celebrities in the mall with people around staring at us from time to time as if they were waiting for our next live ordeal.

As days passed, Aryan got famous, rather infamous, as a gay in the girls' hostel. No girl in the institute shared even a word with him. Nonetheless, it did not affect him as his philosophy of life was '*IIT-girls-no-chance!*' But this slander did no good to his reputation. The girls tarnished his image even on the internet since Swati and her mates posted several comments about him and his orientation in various communities on Orkut. The passing time increased Aryan's frustration and he wanted to prove that he too was the *worshipper of the fairer sex* to all of them.

Anuj felt an inherent repulsion against all the girls of the college. '*IIT girls-no-chance!*' soon became his part of philosophy too. For a guy who had cut just 18 cakes since the time he was parceled to this planet, finding *the perfect girl* turned out to be a difficult task – much more difficult than he had presumed.

I was glad that my jaw just managed to escape a dislocation. Reva's heavy hand indeed had the power to detach my face from the neck.

4
The Nikita Tale

"He must be watching porn!" I said.

We were sitting in Sameer's room. It had been almost a week since the mall incident took place. There had been a subtle difference in days before and days after. Anuj had broken away from our group, without even giving us a reason for that.

"In the computer lab? Naaaaa, it is very risky!" Sameer said.

"It is not risky if you use the computer on the sides. Once I opened a porn site and the system got hanged just then. I had to run away from the lab leaving the desktop in that state. I even forgot to restart the PC. People using the computer thereafter must have had a good time." Aryan said.

We had a natural laugh hearing Aryan's twisted tales.

"Desires, especially sexual, can have varied effects on an individual. It can cause him to go out of his mind and take risks." Sameer aired his philosophy.

"Yeah fatty, you are so right. We can see the effects. Your desire to share your bullshit philosophy has made you go out of your mind and risk your life. I can confidently predict that someday someone will punch you hard!" I said.

"I agree with Kanav. Dude you should always carry a helmet with you." Aryan added spice to the mockery.

"Yeah sure. We were talking about Anuj, remember? We need to check what confidential task occupies his after class hours." Sameer said.

"Tomorrow, after class, we are going to follow Anuj and uncover all his secrets. Ok?" Aryan said.

"Ok." Sameer and I echoed together.

For the last one week, Anuj had been withdrawn and reserved. He used to go to the computer lab after the classes and he returned quite late at nights. None of us had even a clue to what he was up to.

~

Aryan was having a tough time dealing with condescending looks all-around from the other sex.

"Damn them! The girl I was hanging around with read all those comments on Orkut and now she has dumped me." Aryan said after we returned to our room.

"You were seeing someone. You didn't even tell any of us." I said.

"Dude, just once I went for a coffee with her. She is from Miranda House – smart girl." Aryan said in a tone with mixed feelings of awe as well as remorse while the painter inside him was busy sketching her image in his mental blackboard.

"Hmm. Hey, have you read that notice about that social night? What's in it?" I asked Aryan just to change the topic to something more exciting.

"They call girls from different colleges just to provide interaction. And in your case, just to let you see the pink-world outside. This time it's IP Collоge. I heard they have some quality."

"That's cool." I said.

"This time do speak up in front of them, dumbo!" Aryan taunted.

"Oh yeah sure." I said and smiled.

"This time I am definitely going to turn this bitchy gang of Swati,

Neetika and whatever the third one was...totally mute. IP girls, just wait for me!" Aryan voice sounded full of determination

The next day, after the classes, we executed our plan. We too stayed in the computer-lab, scattered around at different places so that Anuj could not find us.

I was sitting in the lab with glass walls, adjacent to Anuj and I could see Anuj's desktop since he was sitting with his back towards me. I looked hard at Anuj's PC, trying hard to decipher what all he was typing, but myopia tragedy restricted my mission. All that I could see with my bespectacled eyes was Anuj continuously typing out in a chat-window. I waved to Aryan as well as Sameer and within a moment they came over to my place. Aryan took out his costly cell-phone with 5 mega pixels cam and zoomed in at the screen.

The clarity of the zoom was well enough to inform us that Anuj was chatting with someone named Nikita. This was how the chat screen looked like:

Anuj: Hey baby. Can u plz send me ur pics? U promised dat u wud do it by 2day.

Nikita: w8 fr jst 2 minutes dear. Plzz. I need 2 fix sumthin.

Anuj: Wat fixin? Wat r u fixin?

Nikita: w8. Plzzz...I'm sendin!

Anuj: k.

Now I could see that the inspiration behind Anuj making lecture-notes in short-hand was daily chatting practice for 4-5 hours. The chat did not move further any more but just that small bit of the chat was enough to make us feel that something fishy was going on. Anuj was sitting idly cracking his knuckles after such a strenuous typing session, apparently waiting for Nikita's photos.

"After Neetika it's Nikita. Interesting. This person won't abstain from girls. Bloody Despo." Aryan said.

In less than two minutes, an e-mail notification flashed on his screen. Aryan, with his 5 mp full zoom on, recorded everything and made a movie. Anuj downloaded the pictures and he was quite desperate to see them as I could observe from his chats.

Anuj : Thnx a ton. Let me hv a look. I waited fr it fr so long.

Nikita: :)

He opened the picture and we all saw a beautiful picture of an extremely fair and pretty girl smiling, but the photo seemed to be kind of over-sketched and painted. She looked strangely cute. Aryan did not leave the golden opportunity and snapped Anuj adoring his *newly-discovered-'baby'*.

"Bloody underdog! He did not even mention to us anything about her." Aryan exclaimed.

Anuj followed his chats:

Anuj: U r more butiful thn wat I imgnd u 2 b.

Nikita: Do u like me?

Anuj: Vry mch. U r a swthrt! U luke me?

Nikita: luke???

Anuj: Actually, 'u' and 'i' r so close tht I cn't find a difference bw the two!

Nikita: Flirt! I like u.

Anuj: I knew U luke me! Lol!

Nikita: Whn r u cumin to meet me?

Anuj: Anytym u say!

Nikita: I m dying 2 meet u.

Anuj: Me 2.

The girl was more desperate than Anuj himself. We were baffled by the kind of friend she was to Anuj. They hadn't met even once and they were flirting with each other like they were a couple. A despo meets a despo - a match made in heaven.

"Let us poke Anuj about the thing now." Sameer said.

"Wait for sometime. If we taunt him now, he would be embarrassed in front of so many outsiders. We will ask about everything when he comes back to the hostel." I said.

"You talk sense man! But Anuj needs to be punished for hiding such a thing from us – his so-called best friends. Let him come, I'll take his class." Aryan said with a demonic laughter acting as a suffix to his statement.

"What are you going to do?" I asked.

"Just wait and watch." Aryan said.

We did not stay in the computer lab for any more time. We gave Anuj some privacy to talk to his *newly found darling* while our trio executed the evil strategy carefully crafted by Aryan.

At his usual time, i.e., 10 in the night, Anuj returned to the room. Sameer, Aryan and I were hiding under Anuj's bed from 9.55 pm, just to see his reaction at the time he would enter the room. As soon as Anuj turned the lights on, he was bewildered. The snaps of Anuj adoring Nikita's portrait embellished the wall. We could see a shiver running down Anuj's body through his legs to the ground.

He jumped on his bed and snapped off the picture from the wall, and instantaneously, Sameer appeared out of nowhere in front of him.

"Anuj, what are you hiding in your hand?" Sameer pulled Anuj's legs. He had been holding the snapped off picture in his hand.

"It was you, rascal!" Anuj pulled Sameer by his collar.

"She is dying to meet you!" Aryan commented while still under the bed leaving Anuj puzzled. We popped out of the bed.

"Bloody scoundrels! How could you do this to me? You are spying on my personal life." Anuj was just one slap short of crying.

Neither of us had a *girl dying to meet us* at our disposal. How could we know what was the meaning of personal life? It takes experience to act rationally, after all. Even though Aryan had the experience, he was not sensitive enough to feel the impact of our evil-plan on Anuj.

"I am sorry on behalf of the three of us. We did not intend to hurt you. We just thought you would not hide from us the fact that you found yourself a girlfriend." I said.

"I was going to tell you about her once I had met her. She is not yet my girlfriend, but I am just one step short of having one."

"Who is she? How did you get to know her?" I asked.

"That's a long story. I was just flipping through the web-pages of my school's community on Orkut. There amidst all the guys, was this girl with profile name 'Nikita: Waiting for someone special'. I just scrapped her '*How come you are a member of a boys' school community*'. And that was the beginning of our talks. I added her as a friend and then daily after classes I used to chat with her. As days passed, our talks became personal. She told me everything about herself right from her life to her family and all that. I find her very much like me."

"You sex-deprived dog! You lost yourself for her in just a few chats. Haven't you had enough experience with Neetika that you found yourself...a Nikita?" Aryan chided.

Anuj started crying.

"Cheer up man. Aryan, stop being a snob and you Anuj, stop being a child! Anuj, cheer up man...c'mon tell me what does she do?" I asked.

"She is currently dropping a year for JEE and taking coaching." Anuj said, said apparently burying his emotional outbreak deep inside. His eyes clearly showed excitement while talking about her.

"I can see that she is preparing hard spending hours on net with an able mentor like you. Why don't you coach her for IIT and then be settled for the rest of the three years of your stay here?" Sameer said sarcastically.

"Stop guys!" I shouted to make the sarcasm kings stop their on-going practice. Anuj being a sentimental duffer would not be able to take on the kind of sarcasm they offered.

All of us were however disgusted with the kind of thing a gullible guy like Anuj was indulging himself in. But we did not want to hurt his emotions. So we beheld our tongues from giving him any piece of advice.

"Don't you have her mobile number?" I asked.

"I have it but she asked me not to call her these days as her parents mind her talking to guys."

"When are you going to see her, Anuj?" Aryan asked quite genuinely this time.

"Tomorrow, in the morning at 11. It's Saturday, both of us have a day off!" His excitement was back to the original place.

"Cool man. Hope you have a good time. All the best." We wished Anuj luck and went back to our individual butt-parking stations.

Saturday, being a weekend, was the day of relinquishing all the stresses we had stored in our body during the tiresome weekdays. None of us would get up before the 'a' of the a.m. got replaced by a 'p'.

I got up at 12.30 pm, fully rejuvenated. Aryan was still getting a full body massage on his one foot thick ultra-comfortable mattress. I rocked Aryan's body to let him lose his unconsciousness. Aryan got up after about a dozen shakes.

After freshening up, the first thing I did was that I slammed my neighbour's door. Expecting Sameer to open the door, since Anuj must be relishing the first date of his life, I shouted, "Fatty, get up! Water would be over otherwise."

The door opened.

"Anuj, what are you doing here? You did not go for your date?" I asked.

"Nikita was ..." Anuj started sobbing. His sob sublimated Sameer's *slumber-turned-siesta* and magnetically pulled Aryan from the washroom with his task yet undone towards our neighbourhood.

"Are you going to say the thing?" I asked irritably.

"Tell us the whole story." Sameer, standing with the support of wall being half-asleep, asked lazily.

"We planned to meet at the Moti Bag bus stop at 11 in the morning. As always, I got up late at 10 o' clock and had to rush to the place. I reached the bus stop on the other side of the road at 11:05 am and I could see just one girl at the opposite bus stand."

"Was she Nikita?" I asked, my curiosity was climbing the charts.

"That girl was darker than the colour of my elbow and had numerous filthy piercings in her ears and eyebrows. Confused, seeing no Nikita around, I called her number. And then was the climax, the same girl at the bus stop picked up the phone."

"Nikita was a faker. The photo that she sent was photoshopped. She was not a beauty. She more or less looked like a whore."

"Did you meet her then?" Sameer asked with great anxiety.

"Are you mad? I took an auto and returned immediately. I discarded my sim and even deleted my Orkut account to get rid of her."

Aryan started laughing uncontrollably. His laugh induced laughter in each one of us, even Anuj was laughing after being relieved from his *used-to-be heartthrob* Nikita. He was glad that the sarcasm kings didn't start again.

"I now know what to do! I will stick to Aryan, this person is going to take me to heaven!" Anuj said.

"Anuj, you are mistaken! I am not of that orientation who could take you to heaven!" Aryan replied.

"You don't know your potential. Just being with you would find me my soul-mate." Anuj said.

Anuj was right. Aryan's personality drew attention from each and every girl who happened to cross his magnetic field except *the IIT-girls* of course. And if you are with him, then you too get an eye once in a while.

5
The Pairing Instincts

Minis, micros and one-piece flocked our hostel basement. The number of legs I saw that day outnumbered the number of girls I had talked to in my entire life. It just took 400 bucks out of my pocket to have a glimpse of about 100 pairs of sexy legs. I was quite nervous since I had never seen such a diverse conglomeration of girls. Girls and those too beautiful girls are the most difficult species to handle with no experience. *How would I initiate a conversation? How would the other person react?*

On the board, it said,

"ZANSKAR HOSTEL WELCOMES THE GIRLS FROM IP COLLEGE FOR THIS SOCIAL NIGHT."

"Oh my God. This is heaven." Anuj exclaimed seeing a herd of nymphets.

"Control man! This is just the beginning. You haven't seen the north campus. Once you see it then your tongue will be tired repeating *'Oh my God'*." Aryan shared his vital experiences of Delhi and then started looking around. He was eyeing the most stunning girl present in the gathering. She too gave him occasional glimpses.

"Where is Sameer?" I asked to break the eye-contacts of my friends.

"I am here. Never before this hostel looked so beautiful to me. Can't you feel the fragrance of woman perfume even in the walls?" Sameer said as he came along to complete our group of *fantastic four*.

"I agree! They seem to have bathed in perfumes." Aryan said.

"Isn't it strange that IIT is promoting western culture bull-shit in our campus?" Sameer asked.

"Yeah, it is a kind of weird. What are they doing? Promoting *go-n-bang-a-girl* philosophy?" I said.

"Actually, they too know that the meager sex-ratio would make half of the guys commit suicide by the end of their stay. So they are actually giving us an opportunity, an opportunity to 'grab', if you can understand what I mean. It's not a western culture bull-shit, dumb head!" Anuj mocked our statements with his counter-logic.

"You two stop your fight! This is the time to grab your opportunity." Aryan said in his grave tone making all of us chuckle. He was looking damn handsome. He attracted not only chicks' attention but even guys' attention. His low waist hung on his pubic bones and his somewhat-nice biceps looked good in his short sleeves.

"Hello everyone, welcome to the Zanskar hostel. All the guys, kindly assemble on the left side and all the gorgeous girls on the right side. We are going to give you cards each having a number – red cards to the girls and black cards to the guys. Match the corresponding numbers and interact freely when we announce the number. Then there are games and a dinner. Hope you all have a good time." The compère announced with a great zeal in his voice.

The seniors promised us a 100 percent guarantee that we would get one girl each to interact and if lucky, will be able to go a step beyond. Each one of us was hopeful of getting at least one new number in our contact list by the end of the gathering. The cards were distributed. I got a 5 spade. Aryan and Anuj both got a 4 and Sameer got a 10.

"All those with the number 1 on their cards," announced the compère, "please come to the centre."

About half-a-dozen guys and same number of girls reached the centre and within two minutes, they disappeared in half-a-dozen pairs. Aryan was busy eyeing his attention-seeker and was quite unmoved by what was going on. He crushed his 4 numbered-card and moved ahead when Anuj caught hold of his shoulders.

"Where are you going?"

"Guys, I got to go before she gets booked." Aryan said turning his eyes to the one who sought his attention for the last ten minutes.

"Wait I am coming too." Anuj said. He loved being Aryan's tail.

Aryan moved ahead without even an iota of doubt clouding his confidence. Anuj followed trying to copy Aryan's walking style to perfection. Aryan went to a group of beautiful-ladies centered around the gorgeous and within two minutes I could see Aryan and the gorgeous isolated from the group while Anuj was left alone. Anuj was literally struggling to find someone interested while Aryan was having the time of his life with the girl in minis. Aryan's stint of glory made all of us go green with envy.

"Those with cards numbered 5 come ahead." came the announcement. I was busy looking at my two go-getter friends in completely different situations.

"Hey Bracy, it's your turn. Go and have a boogie-woogie with them." Sameer said.

Three guys, including me, came forward with just two girls coming from the other side. Many of the guys seeing Aryan making his own way got inspired to follow the same and so the number of people appearing at the centre plunged.

Amongst us there was a senior who was one amongst those who had promised us that he would get us a girl each to interact, who after seeing me struggling came to my help and introduced me to one of the girls – who was quite beautiful by the IIT standards.

"Hey, have you met Kanav? You two have a good time." He said and ran away.

Hi I am Kanav." I bumbled.

My heart was throbbing at triple its normal pace. It was the first time I was talking to a girl who was totally a stranger to me. The blood flow in my face had gone up and my ears had turned red. I could not even look at her. I was looking at the wall and talking to her. She would have presumed that I have a squint.

"Hi, I am Rachel. Before you say anything, let me make it very clear to you that I already have a boyfriend and I came here just to accompany my friends."

Instead of being disappointed, I became immensely relieved. Now I had no reason to go out of my comfort zone to carry on this introduction to the level of friendship.

"That's no problem. Actually, I too am not quite interested in girls!" I blurted out without giving a second thought to what I said.

"Are you gay?" She asked being puzzled.

"Yeah…oops...no…no…sorry…bye" I stammered. I was so stunned by the directness of the question that I started doubting my own orientation. I started dripping with sweat and spookily, I ran back to Sameer who was still waiting for his turn.

"What happened?" Sameer asked seeing me out of breath and sweating heavily.

"Nothing, leave it. Will tell you later. It's your turn coming, best of luck!"

"Card number 10 – on the floor!" The announcement struck our ears.

Sameer spiked his hair with his fingers and moved ahead. He was looking good that day. I rolled my eyes to see what my room-mate Aryan was up to. He and his girl were sitting on the sofa with their eyes resting on each other's and knees touching each other making an equilateral triangle.

Both of them looked as if they were waiting for each other for their entire life. They both had flawlessly perfect looks and shared a charm that was quite unrealistic. I searched for Anuj but I could not find him anywhere around. He seemed to be lost in the crowd.

A huge uproar with a background of laughter pulled my eyes back to the centre stage. Sameer was standing there alone and no girl turned up. Actually, all the girls were already booked by some or the other and those who weren't; were not interested *due-to-some-private-reason* kind.

Sameer came back, embarrassed and hurt, and stood silently beside me.

"Guy, don't get disappointed. You are looking very cool today. Just go and try out your luck again." I rekindled his young spirit.

"Try my luck…" He repeated my phrase and went on his *mission-find-a-girl* with new zeal.

My mind was countering a perpetual tug-of-war of whether I too should join Sameer's girl hunt or not. Finally, my reluctant self took its dominance and I decided to withdraw my candidature. I did not have the courage to stick with Sameer in his over-ambitious mission. I chose to be my company for the time being. I started moving around to have a look at all my first-year studs who had found themselves a company – a company quite inaccessible in the place where we belonged to. The

DJ was on and drumbeats of some of the popular bollywood numbers thumped my chest. Interestingly, my eyes moved quite a lot more than my feet.

The legs were now moving in rhythm, some of them making complex moves. There were guys who were quite simple and yet they were having a good time with the minis and one-pieces. There were charming faces dancing all around ready to be wooed but I behaved as such a timid *duffer* that literally my pants got wet while talking to just one of them.

I went to the sidelines and joined the *lost-my-chance* group and started staring dejectedly at the luckier ones and their pretty partners.

"Paper Dance competition is going to begin in two minutes. All those who want to take part come up to the centre stage." A senior announced.

Aryan and his girl got up after their half-an-hour of continuous tongue-twisting. They were going for the paper dance competition. In paper dance, couples were to dance on newspapers and the one who stepped out of the newspaper got disqualified. A couple being disqualified meant that the others should fold their newspaper to half of the original. And this process continued until just two pairs were left.

Seven newly-formed pairs went forward towards the centre stage. Other than Aryan, there was a pair with one person having quite a familiar face, to my shock. Anuj was there with a girl who was a bit on the heavier side, nonetheless she was very pretty.

Music was on, the DJ played awesome tracks and the couples lacking chemistry jumped out of the paper and got disqualified. Aryan, an underdog turned out to be an awesome dancer. He performed complex break dance steps on the paper and left everyone else spell-bound. His girl was mesmerized seeing his flexible-body manufacturing complicated curves and she too complemented his dance quite well. Anuj, on the other hand, moved his body as little as possible while his hefty companion was dancing as if she was drunk.

In no time, five couples got disqualified and just two couples were left on the dance floor. One of them was Anuj with the cutie and then it was Aryan with the hottie. Anuj whispered something in the chubby's ears, hearing which she giggled.

The last round of the competition was left; the paper had been folded to the length of a bookmark. That meant it could accommodate just the two feet of a person in it. That meant one person had to lift the other person up. The *lost-my-chance* crowd became very expectant thinking Aryan's lift of his girl with the minis would give them a delightful sight.

As the music was turned on, something extraordinary occurred, Aryan did not lift the girl since she was wearing a mini and they intentionally lost in just five seconds while Anuj was in the air, apparently on cloud 9, since his *cutie-pie* had lifted him in her arms. Anuj and his counterpart won the competition. Anuj jumped down and embraced her tightly.

The whole crowd howled; most of them were having a glimpse of public display of affection for the first time in their life. The initial howl was silently transformed into applause. The two complemented each other; after all convex could only accommodate concave perfectly.

Anuj took a break from his partner and came towards me.

"Hey Man, congrats. You two rocked it. What's her name?" I asked Anuj.

"She is Niti. Kindly don't tell her about Neetika or Nikita, please. And tell the same to both Aryan as well as Sameer." Anuj requested me.

"Don't worry we won't do it." I reassured him.

Sameer was heading his steps towards us. His face looked exhausted and horrified.

"Hey buddy, you look haunted?" I asked.

"Ten. I asked ten girls for a dance and all of them negated. Is the word 'creep' stamped on my forehead?" Sameer asked irritably.

"No there is a statement 'I am gay!' stamped on your forehead." Anuj said. Now it was his turn to take revenge from the former sarcasm-king.

"No, that's stamped on Aryan's head and even on his back!" I joked remembering the Mall incident.

"That was not funny, just see him now. Anyway, why did the girls negate you?" Anuj asked Sameer.

"Some were committed, some were busy on phone and some were sarcastic saying I was too big for them." Sameer recalled blushing and getting annoyed at the same time. His eyes kept drifting towards Aryan and his partner.

"Didn't you tell them that you are *small* inside?" Anuj carried forward the sarcasm.

"Shut up! I am already screwed up. See that dog; he got the best girl around. And you, you turned out to be a stud! Underdog, you could not even help your roommate find a mate." Sameer said to Anuj.

"Better luck next time. I am going back to Niti. Remember what I had said, no mention of Neetika or Nikita when I come back with her." Anuj said.

"No Neekita or Nitika. Only Niti." I said. Anuj went back to her victory-charm.

"Hey let us go to him. His partner is very sexy, man!" Sameer asked me. He had been enviously eyeing Aryan's girl for the last five minutes. We went towards *the couple of the hour.*

"Hii. Congrats to both of you. You two complement each other." Sameer said.

"Thanks. She is Riya and these are my best friends Sameer and Kanav."

Riya said a faintly audible 'Hii' to all of us.

"Do you have some friends? Who look like you?" Sameer asked. We thought he was joking, but he turned out to be serious.

"You can't mend." Aryan chided while Riya was laughing.

"Hi guys! This is Niti." Anuj came and joined the group.

"*Niti-ka…naam bahot acha hai.*"(Niti's name is too good.) Sameer taunted. Anuj stared back hard at Sameer and begged for his mercy.

We all had dinner together – the dinner which consisted of just a burger and a cold-drink. Inwardly, I felt quite uncomfortable in their company since neither did I have any girl by my side nor did I have anything interesting to talk about. They were talking and laughing while I was just a dumb spectator busy with the burgers and the inferiority complex clouding my mind.

Any interesting thing I thought I would say, would be spoken by somebody else before it tried to come out of my mouth. Even Sameer had this ability in him of sparking off really interesting conversations. *I wondered why he got rejected so many times.*

Sameer, nonetheless, switched on his philosophy-radio once in a while and spent the rest of the time adoring the *Aryan's-beauty.*

"Happiness is such a beautiful thing that it never requires a reason.

See, you are smiling, Aryan is smiling, Anuj is smiling, Nikita...oh...sorry...Niti is smiling, I am smiling and Kanav – Oh he looks better without his smile." Sameer said looking at Riya and then at me. Sameer's slapstick humour pervaded through the whole bunch and they burst out in violent laughter.

Though I faked laughter to join the company, but I was in rage. I did not like this part of the conversation when they ridiculed my *brace-ified* face. Happiness definitely required a reason for me – the absence of Sameer from the scene.

Much to my relief, the short dinner consisting of few burgers and patties got over and the good-looking flock went back home – and I went back to my hostel room.

I was back to my room and Sameer followed.

"Both our room-mates accomplished something today and we just wasted our 400 bucks in vain." Sameer brought more remorse in me. Though he was a miser, this time he did speak right. A wave of self-hate travelled through my body. Money was not the thing that bothered me, but my low self-confidence pinched me hard.

Sameer left my room after a while and luckily he did not ask about my bizarre experience of the social night. Aryan came back late at night, he was tired, probably due to relating his extraordinary *right-girl-hunt* to all the hostel-mates.

At 4 in the morning, my *about-to-blast* bladder woke me up from a deep slumber and in partial sleep I went to the loo. Anuj was in the balcony, on phone. I returned to the room and in the darkness, I could see Aryan holding something luminous to his ears. He too was on phone. He was talking, precisely whispering, to Riya.

I went back to bed and no matter how hard I tried to sleep, Aryan's whispers hindered the process. I switched off my fan and then tried to listen to all the private emotions being transferred through the wireless connection. He talked about when they were going to meet next and what they were going to do. He was heading in the direction of love; I don't know why but I was very envious. He had at last found his third girlfriend – the lucky one!

6 The Tough Phase

"I don't know why I feel something is missing in my life." I said to Sameer.

The past few weeks had been difficult for me. My all-time buddy Aryan got cut-off. All the time that he had free would either be spent on phone or be shared with his newly discovered soul-mate Riya. Sameer had a similar situation with his room-mate Anuj, who was more-or-less busy with his *intersection-of-Neetika-n-Nikita.* Every second day meant a date for them.

All of the time when I was free, Sameer's crappy philosophy entertained me thoroughly. Sometimes he did talk sense. After all, someone is better than no-one and we indeed were good friends, until he started his gibberish.

"You know why that occurs. That occurs if one has no purpose in life. God has sent everyone of us with a definite purpose in life, which only few of us realize and…"

"Have you realized your purpose of life?" I interrupted Sameer. I was cursing myself having said a philosophical sentence earlier.

"Yeah. I want to become a self-improvement expert, much like Shiv Khera so that I can motivate people and make them happy."

"Oh really, that *'make them happy'* part is so humanitarian." I said sarcastically.

"Yeah, I know that I have the knowledge as well as the skill to bring a change in the masses." He said with his face shining as though he was selected to hoist the flag on the Republic Day.

"Yeah, I do feel that." I said faking a serious face. Seriously, he had the power to motivate people, motivate them to sleep, in particular.

"Do you know what Aryan wrote in that Orkut community in reply to his slander?" I intentionally changed the topic of discussion from Sameer's self-praise to something else.

"No, he wrote something, that's great. The girls ought to be scolded for their immature act. What did he write by the way?" Sameer asked.

"He wrote : 'I am gay. I never had been so gay before. After all, I am in love. With Riya. She is smart and beautiful. Strikingly gorgeous and none of you can compete with her beauty or intellect.'"

"Awesome man! He slapped it hard on those ladies." Sameer said.

Days passed by quite uneventfully. It was around late November, 2007. The countdown for the exams had started. No events of *bhow-bhow* took place in the lectures ever after since Aryan and Anuj became a memory of the past in the lecture theatres. Late night talks and morning sleep became their daily routine.

"Hey buddy, I am going out with Riya. Please read everything, I will come by 9 at night and then you will have to teach me." Aryan said with authority.

"Yaar, tomorrow is the paper. Do you know how serious a major exam is? Will you be able to complete the syllabus?" I asked with concern.

"I will be, don't worry. I would not be able to meet Riya over the next week; so I need to go to rejuvenate myself."

"Rejuvenate yourself? What does that mean?" I said trying to decipher the hidden meaning in his statement.

He just smiled back.

"You are very experienced, isn't it?" I poked him.

"Shut up fucker! You can't even imagine how experienced I am. You are gonna read all those stuff and teach me later." Aryan said and sprayed half the bottle of deodorant on his armpits.

"And you are going to tell me about all your experiences, promise me." I said.

"Oh yeah! Anything for you, *maggu*!"

Aryan returned at 10 at night. He looked exhausted instead of being rejuvenated. My tutorial class started at eleven. I taught him every bit of the things and finally finished the syllabus at 6 o clock in the morning. Sameer and Anuj too joined my one-night coaching class, while I was midway. Sameer looked uninterested during the whole session. Perhaps, he could not concentrate when someone else was giving a lecture. Time passed and eyes went drowsy with every passing hour.

"Now, Aryan is going to tell us all about his experiences. Remember you promised me, Aryan." I said to prevent anybody from sleeping. It was already 6.30 in the morning.

"Oh really? I have no stories in particular. You people ask and I will answer. I won't answer more than three questions. One for each one of you." Aryan said, bringing a sleep-whirling ending to the tiring seven hours tutorial.

"When was your first kiss?" I came out with a question out of the blues. Sameer's uninterested face soon brightened up with enthusiasm.

"When I was in class 10. She was in grade 9. It was in the ladies' toilet of my school."

"Didn't you go a step beyond?" Anuj asked. His face was flushed with curiosity.

"The sweeper caught us and called the teachers. We both had to leave the school after that. She left Delhi and I lost contact with her thereafter." Aryan said with a hint of a wild smile on his face. It was the first time that he shared stories of his glorious past with all of us. He was happy; after all he had found his love – for the third time.

"Are you a virgin?" Sameer hit the bull's eye with his straight-forward question.

"I am a virgin, but my fingers aren't!" Aryan spoke plainly.

My sleepy psyche was shaken out of sleep. It took me quite some time to get the meaning of what Aryan said. Sameer's eyes were ready to pop out of his skull. Anuj, with his mouth open and tongue coming out in anxiety, seemed as if he was tasting air with his tongue. All of us were *listening* with our eyes wide open.

"Damn man! When...When did it happen?" Anuj exclaimed breaking the 20 seconds long pause. He was more excited than he would have been if Pamela Anderson asked him out for a date.

"Three questions over. I am going to sleep."

The day of the exam arrived, undoubtedly the most atrocious day in anybody's college life.

"8 o clock. Room no. MS 420." Aryan shouted while we were brushing our teeth. The MS in his statement didn't mean Micro Soft but it referred to the Multi-Storied Academic building of the institute.

"It is already 7:40. Hurry up guys!" Sameer shouted from inside the loo.

"You hurry up shit-ball!" Aryan shouted with his tooth-paste laden mouth. We left for college, grabbing a bread-marmalade from the hostel mess.

"Where is Anuj? Did you wake him up?" I asked Sameer.

"Yeah I did. He was in the washroom, adjacent to mine. He will reach, don't worry!" Sameer reassured. I nonetheless called him, but he didn't pick up the phone.

I thought, *"Probably he is on the way that's why he didn't pick up the phone!"*

Exams started. The chilling cold of Delhi hardened our asses and made it quite difficult to sit comfortably on the frozen steel benches. Last day study and last hour revision made me quite comfortable with the paper. Out of 9 questions, I happily solved six. While solving the next three, my drowsiness took charge of my body. Eyes automatically shut down and ceased to work. The other three questions were more or less incomplete.

"Anuj Roy." The invigilator announced to which there was no response. My drowsiness was dissolved in a second. *Where the hell was Anuj?* I could see Aryan and Sameer equally worried for him. Just half an hour was left and there was no sign of Anuj.

"Sir, may I come in? Anuj Roy." Anuj was at the door just then. The invigilator rushed to him with the papers and even allotted him 10 minutes extra since he looked quite sick. I could not decipher a reason why he looked like a swollen cake.

We finished our paper and went out, while Anuj still had those extra minutes to fight back.

"Man, how would he manage a two-hours paper in just forty minutes?" Sameer asked in concern.

"Where the hell was he?" Aryan said in a nettled tone.

"Don't know! Is he not well? But he was well until the morning." I stated.

"Wait for ten minutes, we will get to know everything. By the way, thanks Kanav. You are not useless! Almost all the questions came from what you taught us. Isn't it Sameer?" Aryan said.

"Hmm...Oh...yeah! Thanks Kanav. My exam went exceedingly well." Sameer said. He hadn't listened to any of the things I had said the day before and his faltering tone clearly gave the hint that he was lying.

The same group of girls passed by, all of them casting a ghastly look at Aryan. His stupendous feat over the internet a week before had severely poked them. Aryan smiled back to them sarcastically and then winked at us.

"Hi guys. How was the paper?" Anuj came from behind and asked all of a sudden.

"Good. How about you?" I asked.

"Six questions - Forty minutes. What more can you expect? The paper was easy however." Anuj shrugged his shoulders.

"Six questions. That's good man! Even I could solve just seven of them." I said, literally in shock. Anuj was definitely very sharp and had great grasping power. He managed everything in such little time.

"Yeah, that's commendable. By the way, why were you late?" Sameer asked with concern.

"Guys, I bet you won't believe it for sure. I slept off in the loo."

"Oh fuck!" Aryan exclaimed in shock which merged into a laugh. A wild laugh. His 'fuck' was so loud that it turned a dozen heads towards him.

"Man, I told you would not believe it. I slept for almost an hour in the loo and the mosquitoes ate up my entire face as well as the butt. That's why my face is a bit swollen and the teacher mistook it for chicken pox." Anuj said.

We laughed aloud and the girls around thought that we were

laughing at them. Laughter is a strange thing – one cannot differentiate if someone is laughing *at something* or *at someone.*

The exams went on one by one. None of them went splendid, courtesy to the nights out and sleep attacks during the morning. Anuj was given special attention, especially when he was in the loo. Sameer's answer after every exam was, "My exam went exceedingly well." His philosophy lessons went on a week-long hibernation since I took him over with the academic classes. The latter-coaching sessions got tired of Aryan's *three-questions-rule* and we preferred *enticing* videos on the hostel LAN to kick out any signs of sleep, if present.

The whole examination was more-or-less a roller coaster ride for us, providing bumps and jerks all through the way and finally landed us in a pool of mud – the mud consisting of grades, negative marking and impression on teachers as the basic ingredients.

<u>Around mid-December 2007</u>

"Grades are out on the net." The news spread through all the rooms of the hostel.

For the first time, one could see the real use of internet taking place in the hostel. All the pleasurable videos, LAN games and movies were on pause in the laptops adorning the messy tables. We heard groans of pain and joy of satisfaction at the same time coming from different rooms, and this time not through the PC-speakers but through the *human speakers.*

Grades were out. The total made up to 7.3 grade points average(GPA). I was embellished with a D(4 points) in thermodynamics. The professor, who had noted my name, gave me a zero for class performance. Aryan and Anuj who used to sleep during the classes and later on had become very irregular got 9 out of 10 each.

"I got 7.6" Aryan exclaimed.

"8.2" Anuj said.

"7.3" I said.

"Sameer? What about you?" Anuj asked.

"Hell. I got a D in three subjects. It makes the total to be 6.1" Sameer said in despair.

"You said all your exams went exceedingly well." Aryan said.

"That's what! I can't understand how it could happen. This is so unfair. The professor must have done something wrong."

"That goes on for one professor or two professors. But three of them can't go wrong at the same time. You must have done something wrong." Anuj said.

We all tried to be as gentle as possible. We did not want to point out his own lack of efforts and inefficiency since that would have made him more upset or even angry with us.

"Don't be upset Sameer. You have always been positive. A frown does not suit your personality." I said to Sameer.

"Yeah, these exams are trifle in comparison to the great exam called life. If I am going to succeed at the world level, then why should I even care about all these petty things?" He provided a sound explanation to himself, At least he had this ability to motivate himself.

Anuj and Aryan, though being highly irregular and insincere in the class managed to get better grades than me. There lives had no worries. Good grades, good sleep – courtesy to numerous proxies I had to make and finally a good life. They were far more satisfied and happier than I was. *What had I done all the while?* Either imagined Salma Hayek running wild on a beach or assimilated Sameer's hypocritical lectures in my head. The mall incident prevented any further proximity with the IIT-girls and for the school-girls – my image was of an irksome nerd. *Was it being in love that made them so contented? Was it my bleak-rather-fused love life that had brought so much pain to me? I needed to let go of my low-self confidence!*

Frustrated, one day, I poured down all my feelings in my diary.

"Why am I low?

I am low because I want to be. I desperately need someone to share my thoughts, feelings and emotions. I have become too much frustrated because of the monotony in my life. On one side there is an insurmountable academic load and on the other side there is loneliness in my life. My personal life is totally dark, with no points of light coming from anywhere.

Whenever I see Aryan and Anuj joyfully laughing around, I am encaged in envy and self-pity. The reason for my self-pity is lack of confidence, which results in me taking very few initiatives. Rather than missing an opportunity, I run away from any incoming opportunity. I always provide myself reasons to keep me satisfied. I need to revive, to be joyous and to succeed!

Oh Almighty, I don't believe in you but still out of my terrible situation, I am praying to you. Please give some light here!"

The emotional outburst in my diary made my tear glands functional. Two heavy drops of tear automatically dropped down my eyes and my nasal cavity also ignited the mucus factory. I observed an exotic serenity within me. I began feeling light and optimistic.

Part 2

The 'She' Factor

7
A female friend, hmm!

A month long vacation would be a respite from the chilling cold of Delhi and all the academic stresses that I'd faced. Forgetting about everything that happened, I began my journey back home. I was very excited; after all I was going home after a long gap of four months. The four months had flown like nothing - too much of experience in a short time. I was happy that finally I was going to have a break from Sameer's blatant philosophies. My ears enjoyed the soothing lull that I have got after such a long time.

In partially contemplative mode, I boarded the train – Shatabdi Express – often sought after as India's fastest train. I was wearing my institute's T-shirt which said, *"I am what you dream to be!"* with '*IIT-Delhi*' embellishing the bottom-line.

I made myself comfortable on my seat with my newly purchased laptop resting on my seat. In the relatively cold atmosphere of Delhi, I was sweating - being tired after doing the work of a porter for about fifteen minutes. The AC had a soothing effect on my skin and my sweat-factory workers went into hibernation.

Meanwhile, a girl entered the compartment and sat on the berth next to me. Her looks were well enough for her to be categorized in the good-looking category and she looked smart too. Two minutes later,

"You an IITian?" The girl spoke up.

I suddenly realized my status in front of the outside world. The IIT-tag ornamenting my T-shirt had done an obscure task of giving me a chance to fame. *Was the Almighty bestowing some light upon me?*

"Yeah." I switched on my taciturn mode. This time my sweat engine was not started, partially because of the cool atmosphere and partially because a girl initiated a conversation with me, for a change.

"Which year?"

"The first year. Just finished my first semester. What about you?" I asked.

"Oh, I am in Lady Sri Ram College, third year, economics. Hi, I am Ruchi." She said and extended her hand to greet me. *Almighty's tube-light* got fused just at the moment it heard the phrase – '*third year*'.

"Kanav." I said and shook hands. Interestingly, her being in the third year made me much more relaxed. I was at least assured that whatever I said would not be misunderstood as flirting with her.

"How was your semester, Kanav?" She sprinkled spices on my burning wound.

"Ok kind of. Got a dismal GPA of 7.3." I said.

"Don't condemn yourself. It's not a good habit. You should respect yourself. And a GPA of 7.3 is decent enough." Ruchi said.

Yeah, it's so true. Her one statement had more impact on me than Sameer's entire Ramayana.

"Yeah, you are so right. Thanks." I said. I was feeling comfortable in her company.

"Heading for home?" She asked intelligently changing the topic to make me feel better.

"Yeah. Indore. What about you?"

"Nagpur. The land of oranges." She said. Her every sentence displayed her love for life.

The conversation was just sparked off and it lasted not one, not two but for the whole ten hours of the journey. The initial formal talks moved to informal, to all about past history and future planning. Ruchi was 'single' and very academic-oriented, enough to give a tough competition to the geek-crowd of IIT. She turned out to be the topper of her department, perhaps that's why she showed keen interest in IITs and –ians. I was surprised to see the ease with which I talked to her. She made me realize my worth in the outside world in just the initial few minutes of my talks with her.

Was it because she gave me importance? Was it because she was two years older than me? I didn't know!

"Finally I got an IITian as my friend." She said.

"And finally I got an LSR girl as my friend." I said laughingly.

What I really meant to say was *'finally I got a girl as my friend.'* Nevertheless, befriending a girl from a girls' college is really an achievement for the IITian brats.

Befriending a good-looking girl and that too in Delhi has millions of positive side-effects. It means a constant access to the good-looking and even better-looking living sculptures beautifying the whole city. I was not too naïve to realize this implication of this friendship.

"Don't forget that I am older than you!" She remarked with a chuckle.

"Yeah, Yeah. Don't worry, you will remain older to me, always." I replied.

I did not know how time passed. Indore station came surprisingly early and I cursed the Indian railways for running on-time when I desperately required it to be late. We bid farewell to each other, with our unique ten digits being exchanged and stored in our respective cellphones.

"Hey, please don't call me in these vacations. My parents don't quite appreciate me talking to guys. You know they are a bit conservative." She said.

"Ok. No problem. The same is the case at my home too. Don't worry. It was a pleasure meeting you. Do give me a call when you get back to Delhi." I said with a giggle outlining the bye.

The days at home were quite enchanting. Mom, Dad and Sis were happy as never before. The pride in having their IITian son back home meant something big for them. The first task that I did was I added Ruchi to my friends' list in social networking sites. Meanwhile, numerous juniors and IIT aspirants flooded my home to share my experience of IIT. Bored of them, I started a blog titled "Synergy" to let them know my experiences – the mentionable ones, to be particular.

My Orkut account suddenly observed an increase in scraps with about 2000 scraps in just thirty days. The credit for the thousand of them went to Ruchi, of course. Our talks had gone so informal that I was shocked seeing how frank I had become. I teased her a lot with the name of Siddharth, her crush since schooldays. I even started poking her to find me a girlfriend.

The short winter holidays ended and my *mom's-cuisine-nourished* alimentary canal was ready to be taken over by the unpalatable hostel food.

2008

It was New Year's Day when I returned to Delhi. I spent half of the New Year's Day in the train, courtesy to the dense fog in Delhi. The train scheduled to reach at 6 o' clock in the morning reached at 4 o' clock in the evening.

The night at the hostel was splendid, with a DJ around bon-fire marking a joyful beginning to the New Year. I made a resolution in my mind to study hard this semester and outrace both Anuj and Aryan.

Meanwhile, my lover-friends Anuj and Aryan were busy swimming in the sea of love. They found in themselves a gifted swimmer, after all. They looked as if they were born with mobile-phone glued to their ears. Sameer was unconcerned kind – more involved in himself than anyone else. I was there – standing – just watching them trying to figure out why I didn't have any better things to do. Things fell into place and our new semester started with a little 'bang'. *BANG! What bang?*

"A senior told me that the Mathematics professor we have this time is too strict. If he catches one for proxies, then an 'F' grade is gifted to the student for sure." Anuj said. He often heard all these things from our able seniors.

"Anuj and Aryan, Be prepared! I am not gonna put proxies for you two." I said.

"The professor is a sicko man! Early morning lectures, damn!" Aryan said.

"I wonder what a hideous task it is to be a professor. You have to bear all the curses and show some strictness to make people attend your classes and even then people like us don't follow." Anuj said.

"Those who go to college and never get out are called professors." Aryan said in his usual casual humour style. His comment brought a chuckle on our faces.

"Teaching is an art. If a person has the ability to leave the student spellbound then only can he be called a real teacher." Sameer's first pinch of philosophy struck our ears in the New Year.

"Then I suppose you can be a teacher. I am spellbound!" Aryan said sarcastically, which Sameer mistook as a genuine appreciation.

"Thanks yaar." Sameer replied with a smile.

"Sorry guys, I have a call. Join ya later." Aryan said seeing his phone vibrating. It was Riya.

"I am also going on phone! Will come back when he comes back." Anuj said replicating Aryan's actions. Only Sameer and I were left in the room. I was in no mood to hear Sameer's idealism in his own words.

"Do you know that I read a beautiful book called 'The Power of Positive Thinking' in the holidays?" Sameer asked as if I had put a hidden camera in his home to observe what he was doing.

"Oh really. How was it?" I asked with no interest. I just hoped for something to come up and save me from what was coming ahead.

Suddenly, my phone rang. It was Ruchi's call. I jumped in joy to find that my long-lost female-friend returned back from home - alive.

"Dude, I need to go. This call will take time." I said to Sameer and followed in the footsteps of Anuj and Aryan.

"Hey Ruchi. It had been a long time since I heard your voice. Happy New Year." I said.

"Happy New Year. How have you been?" Ruchi said. Her voice was excited.

"I am perfectly fine. How about you?" I said.

"I am awesome. C'mon tell me fast, when are you going to show me your IIT?" Ruchi said. It was quite common for non-IITians to be desperate to see the majestic campus of IIT-Delhi.

"Any time you wish." I said.

"Ok. I will come next to next Sunday. " She said.

"No problem." I said.

"I got to go. There is another call waiting."

"Who's it? Siddharth?"

"It's my Brother duffer, bye. Take care." She said and disconnected the phone.

I went back towards my room and I could see that Sameer was still sitting on my bed flipping through the pages of some of the novels that I had brought from home. I entered my room, pretending that I was still on phone. I signaled Sameer to leave the room since I would now slide under my blanket and continue my phonic conversation. With a great effort he lifted his bulky self up and began to move out. Just then my phone rang with 'Mom calling' flashing on the screen. OOPS! Wrong timing!

Kicking my hind, Sameer left my room and I disconnected Mom's call in frustration.

Weeks later, Ruchi came. I showed her the whole campus.

"Do you know that girl? She is staring at you from the last couple of minutes." Ruchi asked me referring to the girl on our right side. It was Swati. Her eyes were shocked, seeing me talking so naturally and comfortably to a girl. And, I relished that sight.

"I don't know her." I shrugged my shoulders and went ahead.

"This is the wind-tunnel." I said to Ruchi and shifted her attention back to the sight-seeing. Her hair was flowing in the air gushing through the tunnel.

"Wow, it's too cool." She exclaimed pleasantly.

"It's cold too." I remarked with a smile.

The sight seeing continued.

"Ruchi, I heard that LSR has got quite a many bomb-shells, unlike you! When are you going to introduce me to some of the delicately crafted ones?"

"Yeah, yeah, as if they are just dying to meet you. See yourself and then dream!"

"What's wrong with me? Everything is perfect. And yeah, these braces add charm to my personality, don't they? Just introduce me to any pretty girl and see how easily I gather her phone number." I just joked out of nowhere.

"Oh really. You think yourself as a stud? Just wait and watch, we will see soon. Your confidence will be shattered soon. Just wait for my birthday party." She said.

Weeks later, it was her birthday and my presence was a prerequisite for the cake-cutting ceremony.

Ruchi and my friendship increased from the parameter of *'just friends'* to *'best friends'* in a matter of just a few days. We were very comfortable with each other. She removed the veil of low-confidence from my personality and I fell in love with myself.

8
The Advent of 'SHE'

10th Feb, 2008. It was Ruchi's birthday party.

With me being counted in her 'best-friends' list, I had a fundamental duty to give her a somewhat special gift. I bought a nice gift – which was a coffee mug with a bold-lettered **"Best Friends"** conjoining 'Ruchi' and 'Kanav', inscribed on it. It cost me a lot more than my budget for any ordinary friend. But my *stingy-cum-calculative* mind was not activated for people who I considered close.

The venue for her birthday party was some grand restaurant with a bizarre name called *'Waikiki'*. My engineering mind was curious to decipher the meaning of 'Waikiki'. I googled the word and it turned out to be a small island in the Hawaii archipelago. It was really a funny name for a restaurant. I went to the party with great enthusiasm as well as curiosity to see how that weird-named restaurant looked like. My *mess-food-buggered-digestive-system* was hoping to have a good time with the hopefully delightful delicacies of 'Waikiki'.

I entered the restaurant with a decent smile underlining my equally decent face which sparked into a 'wow' smile as soon as I looked leftwards. It was *lust-at-first-sight*. She was damn beautiful! I had never seen such an innocuous beauty in my life. *(Aryan and the company were not totally useless, because over the months they did a sleek task of making me observant towards the charming things in this universe).* For the first time in my life, I was in a party of the beauties, with *her* as the centre of attraction. For a person whose eyes were strained with the weird crowd of IIT all the time, it was a pleasant sight.

She wore no make-up, yet her beauty was touching the pinnacle of charm. Long silky lustrous hair, glistening snow-white teeth fabricating an impeccable laughter and radiant glow on her face left me spellbound. My eyes were wide open adoring her every aspect when suddenly she turned her glance on me.

My *wow-smile-stricken-persona* was frozen as if somebody had made me a statue – a statue with braces. I could not move. My panoptic eyes were glued to her eyes for quite sometime when finally she felt abashed. I realized what I had done; I stared at her for one long minute. She turned her glance away to many of her other admirers in the party.

I turned around to find the birthday girl. To my surprise, every other guy in the party was busy twisting his head towards my *lust-at-first-sight* intermittently. I felt like strangling each and every guy present in the party for eyeing what I felt was *my property.* I was possessive about her; it was the first time in my entire life that I felt possessive about some girl, *interesting!*

Catching back my breath and leaving the ulterior motives to be fulfilled afterwards, I began to look for the birthday girl. It took me one long minute to find Ruchi. Behind a cluster of gift-carrying people, she stood – the birthday girl who got only half of the attention she really deserved. *My innocuous-beauty* gathered the rest of the attention towards her.

I went forward towards Ruchi and stood in the queue of a bunch of *gift-burdened-people* to bestow the special present to her. All the while, I kept looking at the most delightful sight from time to time. Our eyes crossed once more. Again, I kept on the stare until she turned her eyes away, out of shyness or out of social-etiquette, I did not know. My eyes nonetheless were still on her, longing for one more eye-contact. We confident-IITians never leave an opportunity to satisfy our sense organs, whenever we get a chance. *I was glad to find myself in the category of confident-IITians, all thanks to Ruchi.*

I was too lost to notice that the queue in which I was standing now had only one person whose eyes were fixed in some other direction. Ruchi was standing in front of me and I was standing with the present in my hand and my eyes adoring someone else's ravishing presence.

Ruchi was smart enough to get my intention.

"Hii Kanav!" She said hoping to bring me back from that trance. But my eyes commanded more importance than my ears. I was too much bemused to gather what was being said.

"Kanav! Hii…you there?" She dabbed my shoulders and broke my wishful contemplation. The sensation of touch, *hit* to be particular, demands more importance than eyes. I caught hold of my lusty eyes and turned to Ruchi.

"Oh yeah! Hey. How you doin'? Many many happy returns of the day. Here is your present!" I stammered with the shock of finding the queue, of which I was a part, vanished.

"Are you sure that you have brought it for me?" She asked with a question mark look on her face.

"Yes, of course. It's especially for you." I said. I was back to normal, though my eyes revolted every bit of time that elapsed without her glimpse.

"It doesn't seem like though! Anyways, thanks a lot." She said sarcastically.

I faked a smile and tried to control my eyes from turning back. Ruchi got what I was up to. She came to me and said, "Now you can turn around and have a look at…"

"What look? I am not eyeing her." I reacted defensively with my hand*(as well as eyes)* pointing to *my girl*, leaving Ruchi's sentence incomplete. Once again I had a tough time restraining my eyes which were ready to be glued to her - forever. She was stunningly beautiful. It seemed that her beauty multiplied with every glimpse I had of her.

"I haven't even mentioned her. I was talking about having a look at the beautiful ambience of the restaurant. You are caught buddy...tan-tana!" She heaved a heavy dose of laughter to complete her sentence. I was caught red-handed. Her every chuckle was adding a brick of embarrassment in the pillar of my persona. I too started faking a laugh since I had nothing better to do.

I moved to her side to make way for the gift-carrying bunch of chubby girls when she suddenly whispered into my ears, "She is your target dude! You consider yourself a stud, isn't it? If you manage to get her phone number by the end of this party, I would give you a thousand bucks."

Her phone number was enough as the reward for winning the challenge; however no-one minds a windfall of a thousand bucks.

"Get a thousand bucks ready, birthday girl!" I taunted.

"We will see Mister. It's my day and I know that I will win!"

"Miss Overconfident! Tell me her name at least to help me get rid of the adjectives that I have to use to address her."

"Tanya – Tanya is her name!" She said with a smile as if she knew that victory would be in her cards. *Can birthday really make you lucky?*

I just smiled back at Ruchi showing my gratitude to her for giving a name to my *lust-at-first-sight* – Tanya – a beautiful name. I moved around the place, having a look at the beauty more than the beautiful ambience of Waikiki. Our eyes didn't cross again; perhaps because I was no more the new entry – the new-boy at the party.

Miss Tanya was busy with another half-dozen good-looking girls around her; none of them, however, were close to even fifty percent of her flawless beauty.

My mind was busy thinking of the most innovative way to get her phone number. I came up with over seven unique ideas to start a conversation, but none of them gave me the desired confidence, because I knew that meant I was to be categorized with every other guy who tried to flirt with this girl. Ruchi would not have offered a thousand for winning the heart of a girl with a *turn on* as flirting. She must be really difficult!

However, I loved difficulties as long as it was in the arena of girls – though I was neither a stud nor very handsome but yes it was a new domain for me to explore. As any beginner in any field who sees opportunities to learn in every step he takes, I began my journey towards Miss. Tanya – *hopefully a Miss.*

But this time, the difficulty level was much above my capability. She was surrounded by girls all around, and this was making it inaccessible for me to even come near her. I knew no-one else in the party other than Ruchi and no matter how much I pleaded with her, she would never help me. After all, it was a matter of a bet.

Tanya was, however, all that was in my mind, the bet being only the second priority. Her each and every feature was detailed in my mental blackboard. If I were a painter, I could reproduce every bit of her features on a canvas.

The moment I had been waiting for finally arrived. Tanya got free from her delicate bodyguards when Ruchi's elder sister called everyone around the caketable to celebrate the moment of the day. A three-storied cake was adorning the centre-table especially to satisfy the appetites of all the lads and their counterparts. I was looking for Tanya, rather at Tanya and as soon as I saw her going towards the table, I followed her, to finally gain a position just next to her around the table.

The next few minutes were some of the most amazing moments of my life. Ruchi cut the cake and everybody around sang 'Happy Birthday' except me. I was trying to hear *someone's* voice – which turned out to be equally, if not more, beautiful than her looks. She was mellifluous. It seemed that God had deliberately crafted her with His own hands gifting her the best feature in every respect, rather than letting her through the assembly-line which manufactures simple people like *'us' – you too included in this 'us'*.

My hands were unconsciously busy clapping and my eyes were stuck on her eyes which were looking ahead. The summit of her skull was just around my ears, which meant she was quite tall. If I held a meter-long pencil in my ear, then it would have proved to be a perfect tangent to her head.

Ruchi cut a big slice of cake and moved her hand anti-clockwise to let everyone share a flavour of the yum chocolate cake. The first slice fed the first seven people in the circle and Ruchi had to get one more slice of cake to feed the rest of the gang. Tanya and I were at the eighth and the ninth position in the circle. I am so glad that she moved her hand anticlockwise!

Ruchi offered Tanya the next big slice, one-sixth of which she apparently snogged with her wet lips. The dark-brown chocolate decorated her lips and I just loved the sight that came thereafter. My readiness was unobserved as Ruchi's hand moved forward towards me and I took the whole slice in my big-mouth. I did not want anybody else to taste the slice of cake flavoured with Tanya's lips. *I took her as mine for granted!*

I still hadn't got an opportunity to initiate a talk. Wait was what I had been doing and that had been killing me from within all the while.

Ruchi had been watching where my concentration spell was focused to. She took a big slice of cake with a half-palm full of the chocolate cream and painted my face. My spectacles needed a wiper to get a look at what had happened. All I could hear was laughter and laughter all-around, the loudest laughter being the most melodious.

I removed my spectacles. Amongst the blurry faces with *happy-dent-white-type* teeth, the only person who I could see clearly was Tanya, who was laughing her head off with her index finger pointing towards my face. I forgot the embarrassment of the on-going laughter because I was lost – lost adoring her magical laughter.

I pulled out the handkerchief out of my pocket to clean my creamy spectacles, with my eyes still resting on Tanya, whose laughter had now taken the shape of a smile – a lovely smile. As soon as I put on my spectacles, I saw Ruchi's hand filled with chocolate and vanilla approaching Tanya's face from behind. In the nick of time, almost unconsciously, I caught Tanya by her arm and pulled her towards me thereby saving as well as savouring her beauty from any blemishes of dark chocolate. She fell against my chest and then gathered herself.

Tanya, for whom this pulling was more of a shock, was staring at me with her eyes wide open. My eyes reassured her and I pointed towards Ruchi's cream-laden hand to do justice to my strange action. Ruchi gave a naughty look at both of us and I winked at her. I signaled cash with my hand, about a thousand bucks, to Ruchi.

9
Anything for you, Ma'am!

"You don't need those chocolates for your ornamentation. You look good without them." I said and smiled. She looked at me and then towards Ruchi. Ruchi smiled towards us and then attacked someone else who was standing by her side to get rid of those moisturizing lotions.

Tanya was lost, behaving as if she still was confused as to what really happened. I waved my hand in front of her to break the chain of her thoughts.

"Are you all-right?"

"Yeah, oh yeah. I am perfectly fine." She said, after thinking of something for a while.

"Thanks for saving me from this." She said pointing to the chocolates which embellished my face.

"Anytime. Anytime for a beautiful girl like you." I started flirting. It was unconscious. It just flew out of my mouth automatically, as if my mind had a flirting-machine which got activated as soon as I saw somebody attractive. The unrestraint talks with Ruchi for all the while was the culprit behind my outrageous talks. Tanya was standing just in front of me; the distance between us was less than a foot. Her scintillating teeth could make even the Close-up models feel shy.

She did not reply. Perhaps she was pleased, or perhaps not! I decided to choose my words carefully thereafter, which meant no more flirting. I made sure that my eyes stayed on her face and did not move down the neck. After all, first impression is the last impression.

"I was just kidding, do not mind!" I tried to get myself excused for my last line, but what if now she did mind…as I meant that her being a beautiful girl was a part of the joke.

She just smiled; perhaps it was my chocolate decorated face that was the source of her grin. I nevertheless heaved a sigh of relief finding her not quite offended by my last comment. She was cool too, in short. With every passing moment, my fondness for her was increasing.

"Hi I am Kanav." I extended my right hand for a hand-shake. I did not want to lose an opportunity to touch her glowing skin. We finally had a hand-shake, I made sure that it would last as long as I could.

"Hi I am Tanya. So how come you know Ruchi…a..a…Arnav, is that your name?" It was a setback. I saved her charming face from being spoilt and that was what she had in return for me – she couldn't even get my name.

"It's Kanav, K-A-N-A-V. I just hope you will remember my name since my face is not in a state worth-recognizing."

"I am so sorry; I could not hear it clearly earlier. Now I got that. It is Kanav. K-A-N-A-V" She said, her expressions were supposedly genuine. I was wondering whether it was intentional or really she did not hear my name. Her eyes moved to and fro, staying on me when we were talking and roving around in the short gap of silence between our talks.

"You are good at spellings. Nice!" I said sarcastically. *An old habit – all blames to my sarcasm kings as my college friends.*

"Thank you for the compliment. Hey, you did not answer my question. How come you know Ruchi?" She repeated the forgotten question. Her tone was equally sarcastic in the 'thank-you for the compliment'. *'Sarcasm-queen, hmm!'*

"Ruchi and I met in a train."

"Ok, I see. I have heard a lot about you. You are the same guy from IIT who she used to call a Geeko!" She exclaimed with a chuckle. I could not get whether she said it intentionally to mock me or it was just her innocence.

My mind was busy analyzing every aspect of her personality. Though she looked impeccable, my rational mind was still taking its time to examine whether she was equally beautiful, inwardly.

"Geeko! She used to call me that? Now, Ruchi will face my wrath!" I exclaimed, this time not too serious, making her chuckle turn into a laugh. Her eyes twinkled as she laughed.

"No need. She used to praise you for quite a lot of things." She said with her fingers rendering an inverted comma to emphasize her last phrase.

I was happy, because I was getting into the limelight, with my prior introduction given to *the beauty* by Ruchi.

"Really? So finally she did something worthwhile." I said with a smile – a self-praising smile.

Tanya also smiled with her eyebrows climbing up her forehead as if they were telling me to come to ground level.

Our talks were still on - over five minutes by then – I could see with my peripheral vision that the people around were staring at us. Guys must have been really envious and girls must have realized by then that I was a better bodyguard to Tanya than them. My confidence was climbing up the charts, I was almost sure that I would be going home with my wallet containing many more *Gandhijis* in it and my cellphone having the most gorgeous 10 digits ever.

My face was still decorated with the chocolate and I was more-or-less unconscious of it, when she said, "Are you going to stay like this throughout the party?" pointing at my face.

I touched my cheek with my thumb, it got painted with chocolate. With nothing unique to do, I put my thumb in my mouth. Realizing my act being too simple and dumb in front of the elegant beauty, I checked myself.

I looked at her. She was looking into my eyes with a pleasant smile as though they were telling me to feel free in front of her. It was the first time her eyes were resting upon mine during a moment of silence - a ten seconds long moment.

"Oh yeah, I heard chocolates are good for skin!" I joked. She must be bathing in chocolates if that would have been the case.

"Really?" She questioned with a child-like curiosity. She did not understand or perhaps I was too serious while joking! She was innocent, too innocent actually. I misjudged her earlier as the sarcasm queen.

"Don't you use chocolates for your facial? Just kidding!" I exclaimed with a fear that my pathetic-joke would be coined as a poor-joke, as in front of Ruchi, it did. But Tanya was greatly different, in fact differently great.

She smiled and said, "I wonder why Ruchi used to call you a Geeko, you seem to be *quite an interesting person.*"

Finally, I could feel that I was completely at ease with her and her appreciation meant that my self-obsessive ego would be hale and hearty in her presence.

"Since I seem to you as '*quite an interesting person*', therefore kindly wait here. I am coming back in two minutes. Our talks are to be continued after a short break. I need to remove this facial and then you will be able to appreciate my radiant beauty!" I chuckled and she reciprocated.

Happy-go-lucky as I was, I was transformed from happy to lucky in just 15 minutes – 15 unforgettable minutes. Her magnetic presence kept me spellbound.

I went to the washroom and washed my face. All the while, I had been thinking of just one thing –. the friendship that sparked between Tanya and me in the last fifteen minutes made me feel that I could easily get her number; there must be something peculiar with her that made Ruchi to put her thousand bucks at stake.

I came back and was glad to see that Tanya was there alone, waiting for me, she did not go to her group of bodyguards.

"Thanks for staying here."

"Thank the chocolate for staying there." She said pointing near my left ear-lobe. I did not let go of my facial completely. I pulled out my handkerchief, which was already stained with chocolate and moved near my left ear, but could not clean up the mess. I was struggling and finally I looked for help into her eyes.

"Can you help me out?" I asked innocently.

She did not say a word but did something that was more than what words could do. She moved her fragrant handkerchief towards my ears. *What a moment!* In a moment, I realized how important 'a single moment' could be in our lives. It seemed like my left ear had discovered a hidden nose in it. *I could smell the fragrance with even my ears!*

She wiped the traces of chocolates with her handkerchief. I was blessed; the fragrance of her handkerchief was going to disturb me for several nights thereafter. I wondered why she did not resist my request. *Did she like me? What if she did?*

"You there?" She said waving her hand in front of my eyes.

"Yeah!" I exclaimed as I blinked my eyes. I had not even realized that she had finished her work long ago.

"It seems you are lost somewhere."

Yes, I am lost in you. Can't you see?

"No, nothing. So tell me, how come you know Tanya...oh...I mean Ruchi?" I bumbled. Tanya was the only name that was hammering in my mind from the last half an hour.

"We are in the same college. Though she is senior to me, we are partners in the college badminton team."

"Wow. You play baddy!" My *IIT-lingo-used-to-tongue* splattered the short form for badminton quite unconsciously.

"Baddy? You mean badminton." She asked genuinely.

"Yeah, we have a short form for everything there at IIT. Sab arbit hai, I mean... sab arbitrary hai!" I said. She smiled.

"How does it feel to be in IIT-Delhi? You people are the cream of the nation."

"IITD is really a nice place to study in. But sometimes cream also needs topping. Not everything is perfect." I tried to be as nice as I could.

It's not advisable to comment negative about something which everyone regards as the best. Nevertheless, there were not too many negatives that I could count on my fingers.

"Imperfectness is basically healthy for growth. If everything had been right, you people would end up being psychos due to the various pressures!" She said in a didactic tone.

It feels great to hear girls, especially gorgeous girls, talking sense – the delicate movements of lips exquisitely carving out every word with utmost perfection. Everything was perfect in her and therefore I was ending up as a psycho – psycho in her desire!

"Absolutely!" I said adoring, rather than understanding, every word that she said.

"So what are your hobbies? Other than your baddy!" I asked to shift the topic away from myself, IIT and her inexplicable philosophy to the most important subject left – Tanya.

"Hmmm…Interesting question. Let me recollect." She said.

Girls like talking about themselves. Any question pertaining to them always seems interesting to them. But this time the question was interesting to me as well. I just hoped that we found something in common between us.

"I like reading and writing…writing poems especially!"

She took so much time to recollect these two things. *Strange. I was expecting something like bungee jumping and paragliding!*

"Poems. Great! I have tried it so many times. But it never rhymes." I said with a hidden intention to check her intellect. She was smart enough to get the pun.

"You rhymed now!" She giggled. I was impressed by her swift observation. After all, nobody wants a beauty without brains!

"So you like poetry?" She asked.

"*Now* I do, definitely. I hope I can go through some of your poems." I said with a spark in my eyes.

However, poems had always been repulsive to me. No matter how hard I tried to understand them, I would fail miserably. But for the gorgeous, I could even dare to attempt writing one. Her poems must be as beautiful as she was.

"Now?" She said with stress.

My mischievous smile was the answer to her question.

"What else do you like doing?" She asked.

"Hmmm… Another interesting question! Let me recollect." I said imitating her words but not her tone.

I could not mention various eye-pleasing works that my hostel LAN permitted me to do. I began thinking of many of the other *vella-panti* acts that I undertook with great zeal in my alma-mater.

"Mimicry…I know one of them." She said suddenly. She broke my chain of thoughts.

"Mimicry…not exactly. I imitate only special ones!" I said with double meaning hidden in the statement.

She began thinking about what I had said. Before she could reflect on what I really meant, I averred, "I write – articles…articles, short stories and…and for the past few weeks…I have been planning to write… write a novel."

GOD forgive me for lying! I just wanted to impress her. However, I did have a blog which had been untouched for the past one month. I wrote just about a couple of articles in it depicting my miserable condition after getting the grades during my first semester and the hostel politics during elections. Writing a novel, or even a short story, was a thing that I could not imagine even in my dreams.

"That's impressive. What sort of novel are you planning to write?"

"Umm…A love story" I said without giving prior thought.

It is said that *look before you leap, but once you leap, never look back.* Now since I had leapt, though without even looking, there was no looking back.

"Wow!" She said, her eyes twinkling in curiosity.

"But the only problem is that I don't have any first hand experience of love. I need some experiences which can teach me how it feels to be in love, how separation affects love and what change love brings in a person." I said interrupting her 'wow' midway. Nonetheless, I was back on the road of truth. *Quite relieved.*

"Hmmm…so you are single?"

"Yeah and not quite ready to mingle."

"Why so?"

"I haven't found the right girl yet!"

"Ohooo! Right girl! So what kind of girl is a right girl for you?"

"Difficult question. In fact, very difficult. I have not thought about it. It will be an act of serendipity if I find her."

"Act of serendipity!" She repeated my words with great emphasis underlining the word serendipity.

"Are you single?" I asked with an inhibition in my heart. Such a beautiful girl and single, was quite impossible for a person living in Delhi. I wanted so desperately for the answer to be a 'yes'.

"Yes and…" She said. Before she completed her sentence, I unconsciously said a loud 'YES!!!' Her next sentence ruined my aspiration.

"Yes, I am single but never ready to mingle!" She said with an enforced fake smile on her face,

"Why so?" I asked cautiously.

She was getting uneasy; I could easily see that she did not like this part of the conversation. Obviously, it had been just half an hour since we had met and I was still more of a stranger to her.

"Leave it. Let us change the topic. Do you know the meaning of the word Waikiki?" I said pointing to the advertisement that hung on the

wall screaming *'Waikiki'* in bold-italics.

"No." She said apprehending that I would enlighten her with the necessary information.

"It's a beach in the Hawaii Islands. The owner of this restaurant must have lost his undergarments on that beach. Therefore he made a restaurant in its memory – in the memory of 'that lost underwear'!" I said with my index fingers fabricating an inverted comma in thin air to stress upon my last phrase.

She burst out laughing, which continued for over a minute and I was lost adoring her beauty when she laughed. In a way, I succeeded in cheering up her mood. I was looking at her all the while. She was happy as never before and I was happier as never after. Just then, I extended my right hand to her, "Friends?"

She shook hands with great warmth. Now she did not need a conversation to look into my eyes. Our silence had given us a better way than words to communicate our feelings – heart to heart – through our eyes. Her eyes showed gratitude to me for tactfully avoiding the talk that made her feel awkward.

"Before I eat your head with my nonsense, let us enjoy the delicacies of 'Waikiki'." I said.

We proceeded to invoke our hungry taste-buds with the aromatic recipes of the restaurant. It was giving me great joy noting that of the hundred guys around us, some being very handsome; it was I who could grab the opportunity of hanging around with the *center of attraction of the party*. I was making them envious and I loved it.

We talked about every other thing that was at the party and the food, which was just marvelous, considering 'the lost underwear' trademark I bestowed upon it. I was glad that I made myself worthy enough to be counted as her friend. My eyes crossed Ruchi from time to time; I used to boo her down every time and signaled cash just to poke her.

Time flew astoundingly fast. Soon, Tanya's mom called up to tell her that she was coming in ten minutes to pick her up.

I had to get her number, not for the bet, but now I wanted to know her more. I wanted to talk to her, to meet her and to make her happy always.

Just after she disconnected the call, I asked, "Can you give me your phone number?"

"Sorry. I can't."

"Why?"

"Please don't ask me for reasons! I can't." She again was getting restless.

"I won't call you ever, I promise, I just need your number."

"What? What for? Why do you need my number if you won't call?" She looked puzzled.

Should I tell her the truth? Should I mention about the bet? My conscience hinted me that sooner or later she would come to know about the bet, but still, my selfish-mind forbade me to let my first impression get distorted. The bet was not the motivation for acquiring her number, because by that time, I had developed an immense urge to know her more.

"I just need it for times of emergency. I mean…a..a…in times of fest…when your college has a fest etc…" I bumbled all through the way.

"Fest equal to emergency. Are you in your senses?" She asked irritably. She was perplexed as if she saw something evil hidden in my sentence.

"Leave it. I lose…I mean I don't need the number. " I stammered rendering an imperfect ending to a perfect beginning.

I was nervous and a bit shattered with the pain of losing her as well as her number, and the bet clouding my small-brain.

She was nonplussed.

"You are strange. Initially I thought you as a normal guy, but you are …" She said peevishly.

I was glad that she did not complete her last sentence. I had the choice to pick out any nice adjectives I wished to complete her sentence. My mind pleased itself by happily choosing the adjectives 'sweetheart' and 'darling' to give a beautiful finish to my beautiful beginning.

"Interesting! Is that the word you are looking for?" I said.

"Very funny!" She said irritably.

That was the start of the recurring series of her favorite phrase *'very funny'.* It's interesting to note that it's not only her favorite but in fact of almost every other girl.

"See, I am funny too!" I gathered together my lost confidence, despite the lost bet. My ears got acclimatized to the room temperature of the air-conditioned ambience. She was also back to her normal self, with a smile decorating her beautifully-crafted face and her eyes seducing me.

"I got to go. My mom must be coming. It was nice meeting you."

"Just nice???" I asked with my eyelashes climbing quite above the upper boundary of my rimless-specs.

"It was really a pleasure meeting you." She said as she proceeded towards the gate. *The carefree friendliness was back in her voice.*

"Generous you are! It was beautiful…sorry lovely…Oops! It am …I am short of words…leave it…ba-bye."

"See you." She said laughingly.

"When?" I asked mischievously.

"You are the limit! Joker! Bye, take care."

"You too. Good night. See you soon!" I said as she carried her fragile torso away from me.

She signaled me not to come outside to bid her farewell. Ruchi, however, went outside with her to see her off. Her mom would be coming to pick her up. I just wished inwardly that the next birthday of Ruchi would come early.

10 The Hangover

Tanya's absence was felt, not only by me, but also by everyone because now the eyes of the guys were not resting on any particular girl. I lost the bet. A thousand bucks off my pocket was not quite gratifying considering half a thousand had already been spent for Ruchi's birthday present. Tanya disappeared from my field of vision and I was lost reliving every moment of the past one-and-half hour that I spent with her. Her fragrance still pervaded the surroundings. Might be many of the girls used the same perfume, or Tanya's fragrance got trapped in my nasal cavity.

"Overconfident creep! How does defeat taste? I told you that it is my day." Ruchi shook me out of a partial gloomy slumber.

"It tastes beautiful. Thanks for introducing me to her. I had the time of my life!"

"Oh really! Now, relax your wallet. Thousand bucks. See I am going to get rich...muahahaha."

She gathered all her friends around me making me feel like *the biggest loser* alive in the small world of 'Waikiki'.

Ruchi was soon lost explaining the delicate finesses of the bet to all her *chatterbox-kind-of-chubby* friends, some of whom were quite cute. Great proportions of the plump-babblers of Delhi are very cute; it seems as though they had a childhood filled with a calorie-rich diet especially to let them have a non-stop gibber on 24x7.

Meanwhile, I took quite sometime to pull out my wallet. Ruchi, when done with the explanations to the cutie-pies of the city, focussed her eyes to me – *the loser in the limelight.*

"Hurry up geeko!" She said quite anxiously.

Finally I took out my wallet. She snatched it before I could do anything. She looked eager and her cute-n-chubby *something-less-than-a-bombshell* friends were more eager to peep into my wallet – which contained a surprise inside.

Ruchi, with seven of her friends accompanying her in the prestigious task, peeked into my wallet. Just a *v-shaped void* could she observe. Other than my I-card containing my nerdy plus-two photo, the wallet had only a two-rupee coin. The esteemed tag of *'loser in limelight'* automatically got bestowed upon Ruchi and almost all her friends turned out to be on my side. They did not leave an opportunity to transform the birthday-girl into *a hilarious object.* Ruchi must had been conferring great abuses to the bunch of *bowl-shaped-tummies* laughing around.

"What's this?" She asked, quite annoyed at what happened in the past two minutes.

"This is my situation." I shrugged. She faked a laugh.

I had just seven hundred rupees with me and that too I managed to pull-out while Ruchi was busy seeing Tanya off.

"Stop fooling around. Bring my winning amount." She demanded.

"I am sorry. Your birthday present took it all." I said with both my hands hanging down my ears.

"Really? Let me see what's so special in it."

She went ahead and had a tough time searching for my present amidst the heap of big-boxes. It seemed that people had brought gifts according to their tummy-sizes since huge gift-packs outnumbered the small-ones.

She opened the wrap to be surprised seeing a beautiful coffee-cup bearing her name on it, the inscription of my name looking like an etcetera. She was smiling. This time it was not a fake smile. Whatever be her reaction, I was glad that at least my present helped her forget about the bet as well as the annoyance she had felt a few minutes earlier.

"Thank you Geeko. It's so very sweet. You really made me feel special. Thanks a lot. I would have liked it if you inscribed a 'Creep' instead of Kanav." She smoothly drifted from showing gratitude to taunt.

"And Silly instead of Ruchi. What say?" I continued the taunt.

"Yeah sure!" She laughed.

"Hey geeko, I have something to tell you." Ruchi began suddenly.

The sudden advent of news, especially for me, made me uneasy. I was not used to hearing stuff like *I-have-something-to-tell-you* quite often.

"I am getting nervous."

"Creeps also get nervous. I didn't know that!" She baited.

"Silly people do make creeps nervous. C'mon tell me the thing!" I pleaded.

"No I won't. I can't break the promise I made to Tanya." She said.

How loyal a friend was she to Tanya? Tanya, wait a minute…

"What? Tanya said something about me. Oh puhleeeezzz! Tell me."

"I promised her that I won't."

I felt like suffocating her by wrapping her face with all the birthday wraps she had. *Promise, damn the promise!*

"Please!"

"Okay. But promise me that you are not going to tell Tanya that I told you about it."

"I promise, I won't." I made a promise equivalent to the promise she must have made to Tanya.

"Good. But before I tell, let me make you more miserable. Repeat the phrase 'I am a jerk' ten times."

I was pestered and my patience reached its upper-limit. I wanted to poke my index fingers into both of her ears.

"Ruchi is a jerk, Ruchi is a jerk, Ruchi is a jerk, Ruchi is..." I echoed the phrase, the crowd enjoying every bit of fun I offered to them, while I was frustrated with my impatience.

Ruchi broke the ongoing series declaring the universal truth that 'Ruchi is a jerk' with her shrill scream saying "STOP!"

"You are impossible!" Ruchi lost her patience in the ever-glorifying presence of her Geeko.

"Now tell me. Relieve me!" I pleaded.

"Your dearest Tanya liked you. She said you are a bit weird but decent enough to befriend."

I jumped in the air. All my impatience sublimated. Never before had I been so happy. Tanya's face materialized out of thin air in front of my eyes, which were however closed now. My breath pattern changed, I began inhaling deep breaths which incorporated Tanya's smell in it.

"YESSSS!!! Thank God, thank you, thanks all! Woaahh!" I exclaimed.

"How? How could you manage that?" She exclaimed in utter amazement.

"I am short of words. I am on cloud nine."

"She used to slap guys who even tried to flirt with her. That's why I gave you the impossible challenge. I am dumbstruck, man! You would be the first guy who managed to impress her." Ruchi said condescendingly.

"It's my day dear!" I heaved a grateful sigh.

"I can see why they say that 'Opposites attract!'." Ruchi poked.

"She considered me decent, so that means that she is opposite i.e. indecent!"

"Yeah...very indecent! She holds a record for slapping the eve-teasers for more than a thousand times."

"Why does she detest guys so much – no guy friends, isn't it strange?"

"Her mom is too strict. After the death of her father, aunt had to face quite a many hardships all alone. She has become overprotective and scolds Tanya even for any small misconduct and befriending a guy tops the list of misconducts."

"Oh! I see. Now I get the reason. How did her father die?" I felt choked from inside. I wanted to give her love.

"Kargil war. He was an army-man."

"Hmm..." I said visualizing her lonely childhood before my eyes.

"Cheer up, Geeko! You won in a better way despite losing the bet. Yeah, the bet..." She said. The bet cropped up in her small brain out of nowhere. I cursed myself for paving the way for the recollection of the forgotten bet.

"Oh shit. You remember the bet!"

"Don't worry. I will extract my money...Just wait for your birthday."

"Yeah sure. Your memory is sharp, I know, you won't forget." I complimented her.

The birthday warning did not matter since my birthday was quite far – 29th Aug. No matter how sharp a memory she had, she would not be able to remember about the bet.

"Ruchi, now I too am leaving. I have to travel a long way." I said seeing many people leaving the venue after filling their paunches with the yum-recipes.

"Am just waiting for your birthday." Ruchi said.

"Sure…I will wait for you on my 80th birthday. Bring me a pair of teeth to help me cut the chocolates you will be gifting me." I poked her.

She smiled and waved me a goodbye. I was back to my hostel within one hour. The auto-wala turned out to be having a rush of adrenaline. He cruised through the traffic at a neck-breaking speed and made my journey of two hours condense into just less than an hour.

Back in bed, under a heavy blanket to counter Delhi's February cold, I could not get myself to sleep. I was longing for Tanya, so much that it even astonished me. Her face got imprinted inside my eye-lashes and I was wide awake with my eyes wide-shut till 3 o' clock in the morning – an hour later than the usual hostel time to sleep.

Aryan was providing me with unseen company till the time I was awake and even afterwards. I could hear him whispering in the lowest-possible-voice, being capable of even fabricating a '*shout*', from within his blanket. He was fighting with his Riya, perhaps for the thousandth time in his past five-month long relationship. I just wondered how she could tolerate a domineering snob like him.

Does love mean war? If fighting was the end-product of any relationship, then I am blessed to be single. I could never ever shout at my girlfriend, if I am lucky enough to have one or perhaps I am yet to get baffled by this thing called 'Girlfriend'!

I don't know why but I was hoping for Tanya's call or message. My mobile screen looked as it had looked before, in short - blank, nothing new to satiate my longings. There was nothing to keep my mind at ease. Tanya was in front as well as at the back of my mind. Thoughts about her were scattered every here and there in my mind. *Does she like me? If she likes me, then would she contact me? When would we meet again? Why am I so much drawn towards her – is it just her beauty or do we really share some something more?*

"Shut up you bitch!" Aryan shouted into his phone at a volume audible enough to make even a sleepy person open his eyes. My questions got buried in his sudden act. His blanket also could not diminish the decibels by his outcry. I turned my lights on. Aryan realized that his vociferation made me lose my sleep.

I went ahead towards his side, crossing the half-walled-partition between our beds. His face was red and his sound-proof headphones were covering his ears. He had disconnected his phone after his last yell.

Seeing me he said, "Hey Kanav, didn't you sleep?"

"I was in a deep sleep, a sudden shout of someone woke me up. Did you hear that?"

"Oh sorry, I played the movie through my speakers by mistake. The shrill sound might have woken you up." I was just observing how easily he could formulate a lie.

"No problem. By the way, which movie were you seeing?"

"Oh...that...that one...Bruce Almighty..." He stammered. Jim Carrey could not mimic an Indian's accent just for one sentence *'Shut up you bitch!'* However, I was no-one to interfere in his personal life...the life which was run by and on girls.

"Okay…have fun. Good night."

"Same to you."

Lights went off. About fifteen minutes later, Aryan's whispers started again but my eyes were too drowsy by then to be affected by it. Sleep overshadowed Tanya's painting and dreams encircled my mind.

11
Where is my Valentine?

Classes kept me occupied for the next two days. The only interesting thing that happened in the next two days was that Aryan broke-up with Riya, quite late than expected. After poking Aryan for half-an-hour, he disclosed the reason for his latest fight which turned out to be that Riya's phone was busy for fifteen minutes without Aryan's permission.

I tried searching Tanya on Orkut as well as Facebook. But, to my shock, I could find nothing. I visited all Ruchi's friends profile but Tanya seemed as if she never existed. I would jump in joy seeing any new number appearing on my mobile screen hoping it to be Tanya's call. But nothing happened. They say miracles don't happen for jerks. *I was feeling like a jerk.*

Two days later, the date changed to 14th Feb, popularly known as Valentine's Day. Aryan and I had nothing to be excited about. It was a Thursday, the most hectic day of the week, with practicals and lectures decorating our time-table the same day itself.

The *'lucky'* few amongst us*(sarcastically speaking, if you haven't realized)* – who had the fortune of having an IITian as a girlfriend, tried their best to make the day special for their counterparts.

They would use the *beneath-the-table-methods* in the library and make the best use of *the-uncrowded-lavatories* scattered all around the academic block as a mean to express their genuine love for their beloved. On this special day, the lavatories would be converted into laboratories to perform complex biological experiments using ample precautions to prevent any accident. These people are the true followers of the philosophy of *equality of all kinds* since they don't mind using men as well as the women's loo to perform their multi-tasking with perfection.

The rest of the non-single guys bestowed with distant girlfriends used the method of *bunking-the-classes or killing-their-phone-balance* to mark the day of love. Anuj chose bunking the class method to impress his beloved. It brings enormous joy to bunk an early morning practical – trust me – in chilling winter morning, the joy being much more if one bunks it for any one's first love called 'sleep'.

And the rest of the crowd – the majority, which consisted of the under-blessed bunch of single-forever kind of guys, were the ones who execute the sacred duty of marking proxies for the blessed few. Sameer and I were the distinguished members of this prestigious category.

Aryan was above all the categories. His recent break-up meant that his hunt for yet another girlfriend would begin in a few days. His lucky third girlfriend managed to be a part of his life for quite a long time – five months. But the Valentine's Day had something else in store for him. Riya called him in the evening after classes and asked for his forgiveness. She could not consider herself complete without Aryan on this special day. Their first Valentine's Day and they torn apart did not soothe her heart. After an hour long massage of Aryan's ego, Riya was able to convince him to forgive her.

Everything was settling around. Riya wanted to meet Aryan to celebrate their first – Valentine's Day as well as the first patch-up and by seven in the evening my room got evacuated. After idling around amongst the nerdy crowd of the hostel, I came back to my room. Sameer was busy watching some kind of sex-comedy on his laptop. Thanks to his new laptop, his preaching hours had reduced remarkably to a few minutes after the classes.

I lay alone in my bed busy fighting the boredom– being alone and bored instigated me to log-in to my Orkut account. I was proud to see that my scraps had crossed the five-thousand landmark. I could find no-one online, no girl to be particular. Alas, it was Valentine's Day. *But where was my Valentine? I waited for her day and night.*

I checked through the updates of my friends and I could see that Ruchi had added some of her birthday photos to her profile. Straightaway, I flipped through the pages of her album to find that there was just one photo containing the *star-of-my-eyes*. I downloaded the photograph and within a moment, it was the wallpaper – the most pleasant wallpaper in the history of my laptop. Tanya standing around the cake with me by her side and my eyes fixed on her. She looked flawless, each of her features having the ability to make any guy fall in love with her in an instant.

I scrapped Ruchi to remove my photo from her album. The real intention behind that request was that my photo meant Tanya's photo as well. I was possessive about her; I did not want her beauty to be evil-eyed, or catching the eyes of any undesirable person.

Internet helped me pass my time and I did not realize how time flew so soon. I checked my watch and it was already 12 am. Valentine's Day passed without any special gift for me. My committed friends must have had a good time today – some of them might have lost a considerable portion of their wallet, their patience, their temper and few of them even their virginity! This day always has its effect, with no limits at all.

15th Feb, 12:15 am. I was ready to go to sleep with my *five-alarms-and-snooze-on* ready for the next day. I put my cell-phone below my pillow and switched off the lights. Aryan was not yet back into the room – *a patch-up meant something more satisfying than just a date.* I was jealous!

A regular noisy vibe shook my head abruptly. It was my cell-phone ringing. It was an unknown number – with the first two digits I could make out that it was Hutch, the same as mine.

"Hello" I said sleepily.

"Is it Kanav?" A charming voice whispered in a serious tone. It did not take me more than a few milliseconds to decipher that it was the call I had been waiting for days, which seemed like years.

"I am glad that you remembered my name. You are just fifteen minutes late. Happy Valentines' Day, though belated!"

"Kanav, can you help me?" She asked in a broken voice. Her voice clearly depicted distress.

"What happened Tanya? Tell me. I will fix it up. Just tell me."

"Kanav, please help me. There is this guy in my neighbourhood who had been following me for the past two months. Whenever he sees me walking alone, he comes around and passes comments at me. He somehow got my number and sends me lewd SMSes. I have slapped him twice but still he is unmoved. And today…and today …" She started sobbing.

I was helpless and restless at the same time. Tanya's sob was on.

"What happened today?" I asked with my concern rising.

"And today, he gave me a rose and offered me money to…" She did not need to complete her sentence. Her sob increased its intensity. Each of her cry made me more and more restless. I wanted to kill that scoundrel.

"Don't worry Tanya. Just don't worry. I am there. I will fix up that rascal. Don't cry…Please…" I pacified her. My preparation for JEE had not taught me to solve a situation as difficult as that one. In fights, be it in school or in college, I was nothing more than a mute spectator. Fixing a twisted guy like that one required some divine intervention.

"I can't even tell this thing to my mom because her blood pressure would shoot up. She is a heart patient. And almost all my cousin brothers live abroad. I think if any guy teaches him a lesson, he might be in control." She said.

"Don't worry. I am there. Tell me the number with which he sends you the SMSs. Also tell me his address and his bike number, if you have it."

She gave me the number of both his mobile as well as the bike. I noted down. Meanwhile, Aryan entered the room. He was looking quite happy – must have had an awesome day. I was relieved to see him back.

"Just wait for 10 minutes I am going to give him the thrashing of his life." I assured Tanya.

"I will call you in ten minutes. You please don't call." She said as her mother wouldn't like her talking to a guy and that too at the midnight.

"Okay, I will wait. I am gonna give that bastard a dose for his entire life."

I was definitely furious, but equally nervous too. My heartbeat rose to maximum, with mixed emotions of rage as well as fear entrapping my mind. The divine intervention came in the form of my roommate. For the first time in my college life, I realized his real importance and decided to exploit his fluent vociferation in helping my *crush*.

"Aryan, can you help me out with one thing?" I asked Aryan.

"Yeah sure." Aryan said.

"Yaar, there is one guy who had been teasing a friend of mine for the past few days and today he crossed his limit. I need to give him a powerful thrashing."

"I would love to do that!" Aryan said. He was so adept in this task that he became ready in an instant. Years of practice had made him a virtuoso in the field of splattering out.

"You can pose to be Mr. Bajaj. It's the name of my uncle. He is the D.S.P of South Delhi police."

"Who fears a policeman buddy? I will use some popular names which will repair his orientation." Aryan said confidently. His friends comprised all the strata of people – from budding criminals to budding scientists.

"What's her name?" Aryan said.

"Whose?" I was shocked.

"Your girlfriend's?" Aryan said. I liked that phrase.

"Oh, it's Tanya! By the way, she is not yet my girlfriend." I said.

"She will be soon, isn't it?" Aryan said and winked at me.

I shrugged my shoulders.

The number was dialed and Aryan did the job with perfection. The rough baritone of Aryan's voice whirled the heart of that *son-of-a-bitch*. He blurted out at him so furiously that the guy did not even get a chance to show his reaction. I was spell-bound seeing the kind of *innovative-cum-eloquent* tongue at work, with which he bombarded the guy.

He splattered the filthiest of the filthiest abuses and warned him that his mobile number, his residential address and motorcycle number have been tracked and any more complaints meant fatal beatings by the gang. Aryan exploited the names of some of his school-friends who were now amongst the special ones in the famous-gangsters of Delhi. The bastard knew them all, and begged for forgiveness from Aryan. He must have had an awesome sleep thereafter.

Satisfied, with a sense of accomplishment in my mind, I looked at Aryan.

"Thanks a ton buddy. You made my life. I can never repay you. Would you mind if…?" I was just going to ask for something when he took over.

"Yeah, yeah. Take the credit, I won't mind." He said and went to his bed.

"Thanks buddy. I love you!"

Tanya called about ten minutes later and my red-face was brought to the normal automatically.

"Hi Tanya" I answered her call in an assuring tone.

"Did you talk to that scoundrel?"

"Yes, I gave him a proper thrashing. He was catching up with his sleep while I gave him the nightmare. I can assure you that he won't dare again. If he does, feel free in telling me, my Uncle is in Police, I can give him a proper reception." I said and winked at Aryan.

"Thank you. I am sorry for calling at this odd hour, I had no other choice. You were the only guy I knew in Delhi who could help me out. Thanks a lot."

"Anytime. Anytime for a…" I checked my auto-triggered flirt mode which got hyper-activated talking to a beautiful girl late at night – for the first time.

She laughed. I was glad that she remembered it.

"Now I realize why you liked me at the first meet … I am definitely decent, that weird bit could be re-evaluated!" I taunted.

"Ruchi told you about that! Damn she, I would kill her!" She reacted.

"Ruchi can't digest any information. She told me as soon as she came back to the party after seeing you off! Poor you!" I chuckled.

"Why did you call so late at night? You could have told me earlier."

"I did not get a chance. Mom doesn't like me talking to guys. Now, mom is asleep and I am upstairs."

"I see. All the same, I was waiting for your call!"

"Why, for heaven, were you waiting for my call?"

"First answer me...Where did you get my number from?" I tactfully turned the direction of the talk to more formal and less informal. *I was feeling uneasy talking to a girl at midnight for the first time in my till-then–boring life.*

"Frankly speaking, I copied it from Ruchi's mobile during today's badminton practices; without her notice. I am sorry if you're offended."

"C'mon, stop being formal. I am just surprised – pleasantly - that out of all, it is me who you chose to call."

"It's because I trust you. I don't know why but I somehow do."

"I know the reason why! Because I saved you from those chocolates." I exclaimed. She must have smiled, which I could see with my eyes closed.

"You didn't answer me why were you waiting for my call?" She asked.

"Because, I knew you would be calling me."

"How?"

"I sent that guy to tease you. But you were late by fifteen minutes!" I chose the funny answer to escape the difficult question.

"Jerk!"

"Hey I searched you on Orkut and Facebook but to my disappointment, I couldn't find you..."

"I hate Orkut and Facebook; it is a home of wannabes. A thousand of them..." She said with disgust. Her voice clearly depicting that numerous guys around the world had made her Orkut life a hell.

"Hmmm. I am glad that you are not on Orkut." I said in a felicitous tone. I was happy beyond limit to know this.

"A moment earlier you were disappointed and now you are glad. You really are weird!"

"I accept. There are very few weird guys around. I am blessed to be so!"

"A self-obsessive self-centered jerk!" That was the nickname which she coined especially for me. However, I liked the nickname – full of adjectives – because it was Tanya's sensuous voice which was calling me that.

That was our first talk. That loafer did not disturb her again and even moved to some other locality. Inwardly, I wanted to pay my heartfelt gratitude to him for inaugurating the flood of phone calls which were to follow in the future. The midnight turned out to be a perfect time for our talks. Our alternate days talks were soon replaced by daily talks and then the time came when whole day long we would be waiting just for the midnight to arrive.

Most of our talks were late at night, the time when her Mom was alseep. So, it was quite a romantic setting with both of us seeing the moonlight at the same time! In just a month's time, I could make out that Tanya didn't herself believe the fact she related to me on our first meet that 'she was never ready to mingle'. It was a rule enforced upon her by herself to remain in limits. Actually, she had created a cage around herself with a perception that love means suffering – which was fallacious and soon I could feel that she too realized that. I could feel from her talks that she was deprived of love, right from her childhood because what all she had experienced was not love but only care.

Though my fondness for her increased as I began to know her better but I initially dismissed the feeling of fondness as a mere *crush.* Crushes, which were quite a few right from the school-days, often got crushed in sometime and so I tried to wait to crush this yet another crush, but there was something different in this case. No matter how hard I tried to not think about her, I would end up on her in one way or the other. She was not the first girl I befriended, but she was the first one who made me mad after her. Thoughts about her fogged my imagination almost all the time.

As days passed by, the frequency of our talks increased exponentially and Tanya invented some new methods to talk to this *self-obsessive self-centered jerk* even during daytime. After three months of utilising my *Hutch-to-Hutch 'free' talk-time,* I knew her so much better that I could easily sense that she too had special feelings for me. It would be quite apt to say that love popped up automatically. From friends we had become the best friends to finally *'the-bestest-friends'.*

All this while, my academics sucked a big-time, since it was our daily conversations that revolved around my mind all-day long during the lectures as well as the practicals. With my sincere and early-riser *adept-in-marking-proxies* kind of friends around - the kind of guy I used to be - I did not feel the need of going to the morning classes. Instead of incorporating the lecture notes, my note books were home to the random scribbling and innumerable futile attempts to compose a poem for Tanya.

I asked her several times to come and meet me, but her tough home situation forbade her to even think of inventing a way out, leaving my desire unfulfilled. I was dying to see her face once again, to see that twinkle in her eyes, to see her beautiful smile and to be awed by her company, once again.

"**Oops! 'I' fell in love!**" I exclaimed to myself after realizing that the act of serendipity that I had been waiting for had already taken place almost three months ago without even giving me a hint.

12
That Thing Called Love

I was to go back home on 6th May. As days passed, I felt an immense fear of losing Tanya. Inwardly, I knew that I would not be able to live without her. I was even ready to stay back in the college doing some project surviving the torturous summer of the city just for her sake.

I fought a dilemma over what to do and not to do! Two-month long vacations and I am not home - Indore would definitely be missing my company. So many friends, teachers and relatives; I couldn't be unjust to them. Obviously, that would not be doing any justice to my parents too. My Mom and Dad had counted days just for this vacation to start and they had laid their immaculate travel plans.

Travel plans meant visits to a couple of shrines and temples in the remotest places of India. *The places which could take you days to locate on an atlas!*

Interesting? Not quite. These yearly pilgrimages had been a part of my life since my early childhood. It didn't quite excite me now. What I wanted - beaches maybe. *A topless one would be my pilgrimage for sure.*

The days passed and brought me closer to the day of departure. I felt an immense urge to share my feelings with Tanya. I knew that I was going to miss her a lot, since it would be very difficult getting some private time at home.

I could not find a more perfect time for meeting Tanya than 5th May. My exams were going to be over by 4th May.

Talking about exams, never before in my academic history had I performed so badly! Our Maths professor already allotted me and Aryan an 'F' grade since there was no-one to mark proxies. Anuj, however, with plenty of seniors repeating the course got his proxies in place. Nevertheless, this time no-one of them had performed as well as they did the last semester, since this time their teacher i.e. *ME* was unprepared.

"Can you come tomorrow to Connaught Place? Tomorrow my exams are going to be over. I just want to meet you." I said to Tanya on 4th night.

"Tomorrow, it will be very difficult. What would I say to mom?"

"Can't you bunk college tomorrow? I am going home just the day after. Before I go, I just want to meet you." I asked her.

"You are going home?" She was stunned.

"Yeah, day after tomorrow." She asked.

"I will manage tomorrow. You don't worry; I am coming tomorrow!" She said hurriedly, her tone clearly giving a hint of the shock she received after getting to know about my sudden departure.

The day of our private meeting came finally. It could not be called a date since we were not yet sure that we are seeing each-other. It was just a meet. We strolled along the hi-fi markets of Connaught Place and had a great time together with me blabbering all throughout surprisingly. I felt at ease in her company, rather I was mesmerized. Obviously, we shared some hidden chemistry – hidden from even both of us. I was waiting for the right moment to share my feelings with her. Our endless stroll came to a halt when she asked me to find a place to sit.

Exhausted after walking for an hour, finally we decided to settle in the air-conditioned ambience of the Barista. We ordered a *Dark Temptation* and we were getting bored having nothing unique to talk about. I didn't know how I could initiate my private conversation with her. Suddenly, I had an idea - an idea that made my life.

I said to Tanya, "Let me add some fun into our present scenario!" I got up and went to the counter. I asked them for Scrabble, which is evidently available at every Barista. I waved to Tanya from the counter and asked her to start eating her *dark chocolate cake,* which was just then being served on the table.

Moment later, I brought the game-board to involve us for some time with a hidden intention in my mind. While bringing the Scrabble, I spent some time to execute my *idea* - I grouped some letters together and put them in my fist and stealthily put some letters in my pocket while Tanya was busy relishing the chocolate cake. This is the best thing with girls, when food is in front of them, they forget about the rest of the world!

When done with my work, I came back to my seat with the Scrabble and defined my own rules of the game. My right hand was still inside the bag holding those few alphabets together in my fist. I intentionally prescribed, "Only phrases are allowed, as that would make the game more interesting."

Done with the first step of my plan, I continued, "Let me take out some letters for you since you are busy with your chocolate cake."

I pulled my hand up through the bag and gave her the group of letters, which I had clubbed together. The clubbed-letters were L,I,U,V,O,Y,O, E.

Any intelligent girl could jumble them up and make an "ILOVEYOU" out of them. Not surprisingly, I left her no option other than being encaged in my trap. She proved herself intelligent enough as she blushingly laid down the letters on the board to constitute the most awaited phrase of my life.

What more, my plan worked out! Then as it was now my turn, I took out some letters from the bag and replaced them with the ones in my pocket (O,T,O) surreptitiously. The next step must have been the most romantic moment in Tanya's life.

I placed a 'TOO' after that 'ILOVEYOU' and said, "I love you too, Tanya.!" simultaneously, very softly.

My eyes clearly told her that I was not at all kidding and I meant what I said.

The response was not at all what I had expected. She was overwhelmed and got very very nervous. After a long pause, she bumbled, "I need to go; I am not feeling well!"

Hearing that, I became totally numb. I wanted to talk to her, but no words floated out of my mouth then. Two minutes later, all that I could hear was the sound of her footsteps fading away in time. I could not decipher what to do next. *"Time is the best healer."* I thought.

Tired and lost, I came back to the hostel feeling like a loser. The deadly heat of summer did no mercy to me, and I was all wet in sweat all through the way. Perhaps, God liked my *Shiva-with-the-Ganges-of-sweat* version more than any other situation – now when it was not the *fairer-sex* which was playing the role of making me wet, it was the *hard-hearted* Sun.

Sad, I straightway jumped into my bed while my mind was reflecting about whatever happened that day. I could not get what my flaw was.

The thoughts soon merged with the dreams and I lay there on my bed carefree until night.

At night, however, I developed some courage to call Tanya. I called her at midnight – our official time of talk; her voice hinted clearly that she had been waiting for the call.

Being hopeful somehow, I asked, "Hi, How are you?"

"Hey, am fine. I am sorry for my abrupt behavior." She said, thereby easing my pain.

Her apology worked like a *super-energy-pill* for me and it helped me regain my lost determination to straightaway bump her with a tough question – really a tough one!

"You didn't finish the game today. I want a reply to my 'I love you too'." I said with expectation.

"Kanav, I was not prepared for it. I still am not prepared for it. I need some time to think" Came her serene reply.

I had no choice other than to wait for her reply. This waiting phase is the most difficult phase in any guy's life. One has to be hopeful as well as prepared for rejection at the same time.

I waited for days, then for weeks and more weeks to finally a month. *Why do only guys have to wait?*

The day I awaited for so long passed like a jet, with no stints of glory in my pocket. The day of my departure came and I came back to my home – Indore. It took all the faculties of my imagination to develop some novel ideas to attend to her calls. I changed her name from Tanya to Tanay in my contact list – *on both the phone and internet* to make her name resemble a guy and hence diminish the chances of my being caught talking to a girl late at night.

Oh gosh, she took an entire month to think*(after asking for just 'some time'!)*. I had a tough time at home. I had to digest the left-over money after every shopping assignments that mom used to allot me just for the sake of recharging my mobile. I relished every moment I was assigned to shop something or another, since it meant experiencing bliss in a few minutes of talks with her. Mom was also surprised to see me doing quite a lot of home-work during the vacations, quite contrary to my *hyper-lazy-comfort-seeking* self.

There came phases – the essential phases which tried to sew the threads of love into our *just-friends-status.*

First phase consisted of talks – we talked on a daily basis and everyday I tried to bring up the unfinished Scrabble game we had. She very carefully avoided any talk about that *some time* she had asked.

Then came the SMSes and emails, I was the one doing the ho-hum task of finding all the forwarded messages and mails, containing the word "LOVE" in it, from all around the globe. She remained unmoved, but that gave me more determination. After desperate attempts of scratching my right brain for seven continuous hours, I came out with a poem for her, which said,

I looked up at the velvety blackness of the sky
And I see stars adorning nights dress so bright
Even diamonds may feel shy
And then I see one
That breaks free and shoots to
I know not where

Oh little star!
Will you take my wish to her who is so far

Tell her that I am
Just a little lonely here...

She replied a mild 'thanks' acknowledging those seven hours I had put in to make that poem flawless. I felt angry but this anger brought more focus in me. Since she didn't stop talking to me, she still agreed that we were '*the-bestest-friends*' and even agreed that we shared a special chemistry.

Days ran by as if the clock had a train to catch. Even after two weeks, with over hundred *love-is-life-kinda*' mails stacking her inbox, she was quite unaffected! She didn't even say a word about those mails.

How insensitive! I *tried* to hate her for being so mean, but the *try* always remained a *try!* All my loath got annihilated the moment her lovely voice buzzed through my ears after passing through a thousand kilometers between us.

The third phase came when impatience took its toll on me. It had already been a month with me hanging around like a child desperately waiting for just her one word – *be it a 'yes' or 'no'.*

Indore. I was at home – all alone. My parents and sister had been away for a wedding.

I had a God-gifted allergy to these social gatherings; especially gatherings with a hell lot of *backbone-breaking-touch-their-feet-kinda*' relatives. My IIT tag posed another problem – I was to be introduced to each and every person my parents knew, that means near about two-hundred *leg-pulling*.

Even when my parents didn't introduce me to the relatives, they themselves came over to me and interviewed me with very peculiar questions concerning my likes and dislikes, age and future-wage. *After all, for their plump daughters, I was (and still am!) a prospective bridegroom material!* It is a real tragedy being an IITian amongst those few IITians in your race.

First Week of June, 2008

Over the last two days, I had been feeling extremely restless. I had spent over two thousand bucks in the last one month on phone without any fruitful results. Tanya stretched her '*some time*' to over a month and it was too much for me. I was not used to so much waiting.

I thought of giving her a final call. I was anxiously waiting for the midnight to arrive so that I could convey my impatience and disgust. *Either it was going to be my day or my last day!*

6th June, 11:30 pm. Midnight was taking a hell lot of time to arrive. I had nothing unique to do other than reading my messages – the same friendship, love and distance-separation stuff. The *sent-messages folder contained 800 messages while inbox was still at 276. Poor me!* I must have really irritated her over time with my mails and messages but she too was no less!

She frustrated me by doing nothing...saying nothing pleasing at all…what it takes to say just a simple *'I love you Kanav!'* to me?

11:45 pm. My wait had lost its bound, time was at its slowest pace ever. I decided that tonight I would be asking her a clear 'yes' or a 'no'. Enough of hanging in between the two monosyllables. I began to type Tanya's number, when abruptly my phone started vibrating with the screen glowing intermittently showing '*Tanay calling*'!

Wondering, how she could call me before time, I pressed the green button.

"Hi Tanya, I was just thinking about you only. Is everything ok?"

"Yeah, mom went to sleep early today, so I got free. How are you? Alone at home?"

See how she didn't even reply to my saying, 'I was just thinking about you only!'

"Yeah alone! I have something important to tell you!" I said.

"Even I got something important to tell you. First you tell me." She exclaimed.

"You go on first" I asked her.

"No, you go first!"

"Please, you! Ladies first…"

"My news is bigger, I will tell at last!" She blustered.

I was caught in a dilemma – Whether I should convey my impatience to her and spoil her cheerful mood or should I use a gimmick. I chose the gimmick, fortunately, a decision which paved a brand new road in my life.

"Ok, you win. I had nothing quite special; it was just my travel plans. I will be returning on 22nd July, but that is quite inconsequential to you! Leave the crap out...you say!"

"It is not inconsequential to me. It matters to me. So when are you coming for a date with me?"

Startled, I mumbled, "Are you ok?"

"I am not ok, I am in love! I am in love with you Kanav!" She exclaimed.

Sudden unconscious tears dropped down my eyes. Tears of joy, a joy hat was inexpressible, flooded my eyes and then didn't even spare my ace.

"I knew you were the one for me from the very first day I met you, ut I needed some time to prepare myself as well as yourself for this commitment. I just want to say that I love you much more than you love me." She continued.

"All the while I had been fighting with myself about whether I should choose my family or you, and now I realize that I could lose neither of them. You both are my life. Today, in the evening I just had a thought which cleared all my doubts. I recalled my life before you came into it. It had been without joy, without happiness and without love. I used to run away from everyone, I used to avoid any interaction but you still managed to creep into my life. Your innocence and simplicity assured trust and love from the very first day. I so much want to share my happiness of finding you with my mom, to let her see that how happy her daughter is with her life, but alas she wouldn't understand. I had never been so happy before." She said. She was in tears – I could see through the phone, emotionally speaking.

"I love you. I love you so much." I said and I didn't realize the two heavy tear-drops waiting for a blink to fall. I blinked and burst into tears.

I was sobbing, sobbing with joy. At last, my perseverance outraced her dilemma. I was feeling blessed – blessed to heaven. It seemed as if a burden had been removed from my heart. I felt like a child, carefree and blithe, running wild across the meadows. I put down the phone, to let our emotions take rest for sometime, opened my long-forgotten diary and penned down –

"People say that love is pure, love is blind, love is fair, love is unfair, love enhances oneself or love spoils oneself; but I haven't experienced anything! My feelings have not been changed nor am I. I am still the same guy who cries watching any romantic movie, who abuses the Indian bowlers if they are struck for boundaries, who spends useless hours on net just refreshing his scrapbook.... but there is something that ensures an immense contentment

inside me. I am not mad in love, but I love somebody madly.

It's not that I am never sad or negativities don't shoot me because I am in love...it's not that I don't give a damn to this world because I am in love...it's not that I am not affected by the jeers of this world...but it's just that I have a very very special person on this planet, after talking to whom all my pains are sublimated, I become abnormally rejuvenated and satisfied. My life has been touched to the core, and there is a big difference in me which only I can realize.

I am in love; 'I' am in love and 'I' love to be in love!"

My parents returned a day after. Thereafter I had my pilgrimage to Arunachal. For the first time, I had felt grateful to God. Mom was shocked seeing me so devoted. Though I didn't believe in God but I just wanted to shower my gratitude to him. The days after the acceptance of my proposal, were like years for me. All through the day I would be lost in thoughts about Tanya. The wait for the midnight seemed torturous. All the same, I was happy, perpetually happy.

So, two and a half months were well spent at home. Though about one-and-half months were spent thinking about *her* and the rest of the time in something constructive i.e. talking to *her*.

In all those moments of wait, anxiety and finally ecstasy, I learnt a great lesson of life - "Whenever any girl says that she needs time, it is very probable that she is interested." So the moral of the story is to keep trying until you succeed.

22nd July 2008

I was back to the hostel. The end of *my long wait* marked an end of Tanya's *not-so-long-wait.* Not-so-long because she had a free month, which she utilized not to wait but to do a somewhat tougher task. The task of choosing between two utterly difficult words - *'yes' and 'no'*, both having one vowel each. She finally chose the one with more consonants. *A lifelong relief for me.*

I didn't tell any of my friends about Tanya. I was so possessive about her that I didn't want even my friends to eye her, since my Tanya's innocuous beauty was enough to give all their girlfriends a run for their beauty. My room always remained bolted from inside to prevent frequent philosophical encounters with Sameer and to provide me with privacy. Aryan and Anuj were busy with their own love lives.

The Same Day, Midnight

Fortunately, from the second year I got a single room, which automatically offered me enough privacy to craft my *brand-new-love-story.*

"I have told my mom that there is a birthday party of my classmate on Sunday and she has allowed me to go. So I have my Sunday totally free." Tanya said over excitedly.

"That's great! What date is it?" I asked in a happy tone.

"27th July. So here is your first date!"

"Definitely! Prepare to get assaulted." I joked.

"Shut u…p!" Tanya blushed.

"27th July. Make note of this day. This is going be the most special day of your life." I said.

"So what are you going to bring for me?" Tanya asked all of a sudden.

"Do I need to bring something for you? Hmm. Let me think. How about braces for you too? We would look perfectly made for each other once you wear it!" I said.

"Stop kidding! You must have thought about it. Tell me, please." Tanya pleaded. I really had something unique in my mind to take for her, but I just loved poking her.

"*Meri shaadi ka card*!" I joked again.

"You are so mean!" She said.

"It will be a surprise. No questions my dear lady."

Part 3

My 'Special' Day

13
A Kick-ass Kickoff

27th July, 2008 - My Special Day

On your mark, get set, go! With the shot of a revolver, all the runners began running the race. I was exerting myself to my best but I could not move. I looked back and was puzzled to see that an old bearded man wearing a T-shirt saying 'God' was holding me with six semi-invisible strings.

He said and his voice echoed, "Run child run. Let me see how nicely you run today. You've prepared for this race for so long, isn't it?"

I looked in front and saw all my rivals touching the finishing line. Out of nowhere, an infinitely deep well appeared in front of me with hot and fuming magma climbing up. My heart whirled with fear.

Horrified, my heart already started to skip beats; I looked back at the bearded fellow. A dazzling aura encircled His skull and He smiled showing His perfect teeth. His whiskers became radiant in the glow of His halo. Suddenly, he materialized a scissor in His hand and started cutting the invisible strings which were emerging out of His hand, one by one. I was just one string short of diving into the bubbling magma. The atmosphere turned dusky.

"Be careful my child. All the best!" The grave baritone buzzed the dusky atmosphere and He cut the strings.

Huff! Dhak–dhak, dhak-dhak, dhak-dhak, dhak-dhak! My heartbeat was on top of the charts. I looked out of window. I was in a fix wondering how dawn could hit at the time of dusk!

I brought my eyes back to their original position. In front of my eyes, there was a thing which seemed quite familiar. Something that I hadn't taken note of ever before.

I could see a *white-cobweb-ornamented-ceiling* with a century-old fan, running at a speed which could make it easy for even a *cataract-stricken-oldie* to count the number of rotations per second.

For two minutes, I kept my stare on…No, I was not counting the rotations but I was doing the delicate work of lowering my heartbeat.

After playing blink with the wall for about two minutes, I closed my eyes to restart the unfinished task. Fortunately, the bearded man didn't appear again.

I was sleeping, sleeping and slightly sweating...the *tortoise-incarnation-fan* was unable to counter the 7.15 am morning sun efficiently!

Nevertheless, I was having a good doze and that's what mattered!

zzzzzzzzzzz..........................

7.30 am

My phone started ringing with the Nokia tune in its loudest pitch. Unaware and indifferent, I *pushed* the green button with the tip of my index finger.

"Good morning honey, c'mon get up! You have to take your breakfast" Tanya said in a very sensuous voice.

Man, I loved that voice! I can forsake everything just for that voice.

Fortunately, Tanya was one of her kind, the so-called *earnest-organized-disciplined-all-in-one* – a bit uncommon in today's crowd. I assigned her the fundamental duty of waking up a *kumbhkaran* like me daily, marking an *aesthetic offset* to my day with her soothing voice.

The very voice, made me feel more comforted and ironically induced snug and lethargy in bed than ever.

"Kanav, get up! I don't have much time. Mom would come in a minute."

"I had a nightmare. I was falling into the magma..." I replied still being totally smitten by sleep.

"You are still asleep, Kanav. Get up. Honey please." Tanya's tone became harsh.

"I got up baby, don't worry!" I opened my eyes hearing Tanya's rebuke. Seconds later, I started inhaling deep breaths again and my eyes shut down automatically...not realizing that the phone was still on.

After five minutes, which passed like two microseconds, the phone started ringing again. I took on the phone with my eyes still closed, *pushed* the green button again and said, "Hey Baby."

The reply was, "Hey Baby *nahin*, Hi Ma!"

You can understand my situation. The shackles of slumber, under which I had been for the last seven hours, were instantly shattered into pieces. I jumped from the bed, with 100% concentration on my words and senses, I stammered, "Hi Ma...how are you?"

She replied, *"Meri baat baad mein karte hain,* first tell me, who's this 'Hey Baby'?"

Dumbstruck, no thoughts - other than the official four-lettered F word - jumped into my mind for one long minute. I could feel the nightmare happening again in front of me. I felt an inherent dislike for God inside me. His last words, "Be careful son" echoed again in my ears.

Why does this happen to me? Why do I always fall into the trap? Questions like these were banging my head. Suddenly, I came up with an idea - an idea that indeed saved my life.

"Mom, there was a dream, *baś ek sapna tha*, I was hanging out with a girl. I was still in a trance, that's why..." I replied breaking that long pause.

"Something is wrong, something fishy is going on. I can understand everything! Anyway, I know that you won't tell... *Tu to nikamma hai*...go have your breakfast. *Sunday tha islie socha utha deti hun...par tum to apne 'Hey Baby' ke khayal mein hi pade raho*" came my mom's scolding.

I thanked God for giving me a brain that worked at the time I needed it the most. I reflected on the profound truth mom had just then revealed to me - *"Tu to nikamma haï..."*

I pacified myself, '*Nikamme* can also work wonders.' and I went to freshen up. I switched off my cell-phone since I had enough of it since the morning.

The joy of having the eyes closed after a tiresome day with the body lying cozily on the bed in shapes more complex than the *structure-of-DNA* is the most lucrative luxury of this world. I bet you too would never want to forgo it – not even for the sake of *the-rare-Sunday-breakfast.*

Never before had anything given such a humiliating defeat to my sloth. I was standing there completely blank, in front of my bed, on which lay my dear phone! Indeed, it was very dear to me. It had been a store for my messages – all those *luvly-dubly-talks* which initiated my love-life.

My sluggishness had been vanished. No matter how attractive my bed seemed, I knew I could not get another glimpse of *that-perfect-silence*. So finally, since I had got up on time, I went down to the hostel mess to have my breakfast.

The previous semester there was no single day when I had my breakfast on Sunday. I used to get up at around 1'o clock and straightaway go for lunch *(without even brushing my teeth, as water would have been over by then!).* I was happy because this time, fortunately, I captured the rare opportunity to attend what we used to call '*The Sunday breakfast*', courtesy my mom.

After such a happening kick-off of the day, it is but natural that anything that could satisfy my appetite would taste wonderful. I ate *jalebis* - about eight of them. It took me some time to come to the ground level and then I realized that it was Sunday - *the special day.*

We were to meet at the Kashmere Gate Metro Station at 11:30 am, and it was already 8:30am.

Kashmere Gate was chosen primarily due to two reasons. First, it was quite distant from Tanya's home so we could avoid rendezvous with anyone familiar, plus there was a McDonalds in the station premises itself. A big station with platforms underground as well as an over bridge above offered quite a few places to wander about. The over-bridge offered us vantage points to have a look at the *beautiful-cum-polluted* capital of the nation.

To impress my brand new girlfriend, I went for a half an hour-long bath – you certainly need such a long bath if you happen to bathe weekly – and came out looking totally fresh. I put out all the almirah treasure on my small bed and took my time at scrutinizing the clothes I wanted to put on.

"A loose white T-shirt and a dark blue Jeans will suit my personality" I convinced myself. After putting on the attire, I saw myself in the mirror. I was looking really good.

"Looking cool!" I complemented myself in front of the mirror and I took my shaving kit and went on to the washroom with my mind lost in the grip of complacency. It being a Sunday, I was really fortunate since Aryan was home and the whole bunch including Anuj and Sameer were busy catching up with their sleep.

Lost in the thoughts of self-praise, I put the cream on my face. I rubbed hard and got enough lather to hide my entire constellation set.

As I began shaving, I came back from my complacent phase to the present moment because of a peculiar smell that was playing with my nasal cavity. It smelled familiar, just like peppermint, and my face literally started freezing for a moment. It did not take me long to realize where the root of the smell was!

Three seconds later,

"Damn, I had put the toothpaste on my face!" I exclaimed, being appalled.

The faux pas made me laugh and cry at the same time. After about half a dozen face-washes, my horror diminished. I was happy that no-one was present in the washroom at that time; otherwise I would become an object of ridicule for my hostel friends.

I came back to my room and stood in front of the mirror. My eyesight filtered through the great range of cosmetics available in my room. After playing with perplexities for about four minutes, I chose the Axe deodorant - the strongest one hoping that it would do something good in the near future.

I finished half the bottle on myself (from top to bottom) and still was not satiated. I dropped three bottles of deodorants into my bag, hoping that by the time the smell of the first one fades away, I will use the other one. Filling half of my palms with the wet-look hair-gel, I styled my hair imitating Aamir Khan of *Taare Zameen Par*.

As I looked into the mirror, my face shone. Initially I was very proud of it, but then I realized that it was due to the advanced whitening toothpaste that I had applied on my face. This realization brought a tinge of embarrassment but that didn't matter as finally I got something that made me look good.

9:38 am. Fully prepared, with the *surprise* for Tanya in my pocket, three sets of handkerchiefs - one for the nose, one for the sweat and one for the lady *(if need arises!)*, and three bottles of deos in the bag, I left my room. I looked as if I had taken Aryan's mania for the number *three*. I hoped this time there would be no tryst with errors. Anxiety was back in my mind and I was totally ready to attack the fish, with my wallet flooding with cash, giving me a sense of pride.

14
Prakriti's Call

9:44 am. I reached the exit of my hostel, when suddenly someone started calling. Interestingly, this call was not on the phone, nor could I hear any voice. Rather, this was the call of my oldest girlfriend, Prakriti who loves playing with when I am in haste. In moments of hurry, she bangs on the bull's eye and frustrates me to the max.

She is an obsessed nymphomaniac *(she does not leave women too!)*, as she loves playing not only with me, but with everybody, be it a guy or a girl. Her timing is just perfect, as she descends into our lives just before any important interview, or any viva session, or any important stage performance.

Prakriti, before your imagination sketches her beautiful face in your mental drawing book, is really very gorgeous. Most people call her lovingly as *Nature*, and attend to her calls regularly without much fuss. But, when she called me that time, I became furious. I understood that eight *jalebis* had done their trick.

From the exit of my hostel, I came back running at my maximum pace giving tough competition to Milkha Singh. I dropped down *all my stuff* at my room and rushed to the washroom. In the washroom, I came to know that it was not any ordinary call but rather a serious one. Everything I have had since the morning dropped down as swiftly as it could. I was utterly helpless.

With no great work to do other than hearing some really bizarre noises, I used the time to cry out for the last help.

With skepticism, I prayed to the Almighty, "Please save me! Play with me on any other day but kindly spare this one."

The initial excitement was mucked up due to the terrible condition of my abdomen. One part of my brain suggested me to drop the plan, but the egoistic part of me instigated me to challenge God and move on. Annoyed, I began searching for some help on my own.

I came out of the washroom; being ultra-psyched at my dysfunctional digestive system. The happy-go-lucky guy in me had become a crappy-go-mucky hombre. My face was no more excited; it needed *something – something effective.* Meanwhile, the adjacent cubicle in the washroom opened. To make matter worse, it turned out to be Anuj.

Anuj asked me, "Something wrong? So well-dressed yet such a gloom on your face?"

I didn't answer.

"Headed to see somebody special?" He asked.

"Kinda' yes!" I blushed trying to hide my disgust as well as anger simultaneously. I tried to involve myself in cracking my knuckles just to avoid eye contact with him.

"Mr. Kanav with a girl. Ohoooooo!" He stated and jumped as if he was going to make it to the national dailies.

"Kanav is going for a date!" He screamed at his maximum volume, making sure that it got into the ears of all the *sleepy-lazy-nerdy-heads* of my hostel and they could relish the latest headline amongst hostel gossip-times.

The wrath at Anuj's action got concealed inside me since Prakriti was back to action. Her second call came, this time without a bang though. I liked it too, since I was in a way rescued from my sudden popularity just outside the washroom.

For the first time in my life, I recognized Prakriti's spiritual importance. I realized, '*She is God's messenger especially sent to remind us of His Holy Presence.*'

After disconnecting the second call, I tried to sneak out of my hostel but could not taste triumph that time. The whole bunch of the *early-Sunday-risers* was there, ready to attack me. Questions were not what they had to bombard me with, rather it was mockery!

Prakriti in action plus mockery about Tanya made an awful combination – two of the most important ladies of my life playing the game simultaneously.

Fortunately, the number of *early-Sunday-risers* in my hostel was just a one digit figure. Anuj's shout did not have enough decibels to wake Sameer up, our fatty, who would have been sleeping after watching his American Pies for the *nth time* at night. Before they could ask anything personal, I held my stomach in my hands.

"My condition is not good; I need a medicine – which can instantly check my condition!" I pleaded genuinely.

"Wait a minute, I have a tablet. It's very effective!" Anuj said. My wrath was dissolved in a moment. As he went to get the medicines, the crew surrounding me began –

"You got a girlfriend? When? In the holidays? What's her name? You turned out to be an underdog man..." And much more were the questions thrown at me in the on-going localized press conference – that too in the toilet. Meanwhile, Anuj came back with the call-diverting tablet for me.

"It's a long story. I will tell all of you in detail...tonight when I come back!"

"*Banda to stud nikla*!" One of my friends commented with almost everyone around reciprocating in unison, "*Sahi mein yaar*!"

Having a girlfriend is really an accomplishment for the IIT crowd.

Happy to hear the bottom-line with me being the stud, I took the divine tablet from Anuj who had taken a little more than a minute to return back to the *conferencing corridor.*

"Bye." I said disinterestedly giving them a clear hint that I liked to have my personal life personal.

I was spared for the time being. With one tablet in my mouth and another in my pocket, I took my bag and restarted my journey with a ray of optimism.

A bit nervous in anticipation and a bit excited about what was to happen in a few hours, I embarked on my journey. With headphones in my ears, a slight smile on my face, a chewing gum in my mouth and a smart walk, I gave my best to look as *the coolest guy* in the campus.

On the way, I SMSed Tanya, "Hey, I am leaving my place, will be there at the metro station by 11:30. Love ya."

'She might also be nervous and excited, after all her long wait was finally over' I thought. After realizing that someone is desperately waiting to meet me, a phase of complacency crept into my attitude, again.

I consciously set my hairstyle once again and felt '*cool*' from inside. I became so conscious about my appearance that before every glass pane of the cars parked on the way, I scrutinized my visual aspect.

I moved through the way and reached the main gate of my Institute. I searched for an auto-rickshaw rather than the usual blue-line bus, as I was worried not to crush my well-pressed T-shirt.

I went to the auto-driver and asked him, "Central Secretariat, Metro Station. How much will you charge?"

He looked at me from top to the bottom, and then he said, "90 rupees."

I thought, "Perhaps, he is impressed by my looks, that's why he demanded more."

Flattered, I agreed, *(though the original fare was just Rs.70)* and boarded the auto without much fuss.

With Bryan Adam's famous song - "I Am Ready!" bombing my ears in its full bass, a new enthusiasm enthralled me for my most awaited journey - the journey towards my love.

I observed people passing by through my peripheral vision. Even they could not resist noticing me. For the first time, I had a *natural smile* popping out of my face.

10:32 am. After trudging through more than half of the way, with the scorching heat of Delhi inducing perspiration, the auto came to a halt. There was a massive jam ahead and I could not trace its cause.

Perspiration increased my desperation as sweat entangled my cool persona, and nearly whole of my shirt became wet. I took out the *second bottle* from my bag and sprayed it on myself to kick-off any sign of body-odour present.

Realizing that the jam would take too much time, I got down from the auto and looked towards the horizon. All I could see were vehicles of all sizes, from cars to autos to buses to even an elephant!

"How far is the metro station from here? If I go walking?" I asked the auto-rickshaw driver.

"1 km. This jam is not going to be over." He replied in his naïve tone.

"Bro, you didn't drop me the whole way. I will give just 60 rupees." I insisted.

"Saheb, it has been more than half the way, I deserve at least 70 rupees." He bargained.

By the way, I was very happy from inside at this sudden winning streak because I managed to get to the metro station in Rs.70 only. My hand went to my pocket, but to my surprise...

My wallet was missing! Terrified, I started searching my bag and pockets, but without any hick.

I started thinking, "When did I last use my wallet?"

No answer came to my mind. One minute later, when I came across the *prakriti-inhibiting tablet,* I realized that I had left my wallet in my room, at the time when I went back to the room before attending my first girlfriend's call.

I was helpless; with no money and just a bag containing three perfume bottles, handkerchiefs and a pen. Even my ATM card and the Metro Smart Card were in my wallet. Embarrassed, I stared at the auto-wala with my eyes pleading for mercy.

I had no other option other than dealing my stuff with him. I realized that I had to ask him for some money too; otherwise I would not be able to reach my destination.

I pulled out two bottles of perfume and exercised my salesmanship. I saved one bottle of Axe to come to my rescue for fighting with sweat.

I told the auto-wala, "Bhaiya, I forgot to bring my wallet. You keep these perfumes. Counting both their prices, it is about 350 rupees. They are a bit used, that's why I am selling them to you for 200 rupees. Keep your share of 70 rupees and return me the remaining 130 rupees..."

He replied sternly, "*Bhai, ye kya hai? Aisa nahin hota hai!*"

"Bhaiya, these are imported. *Aap fayde mein hi rahoge*. I have a very urgent work to do. Please understand." I said, pleadingly.

"*Ladki ka chakkar hai*?" He said with a spark on his face. His greedy smile added to my misery. God only knows why these people are so obsessed with girls.

"*Nahin perfume ki dukaan kholne jaa raha hun!*" I thought in disgust.

"*Haan yaar*, please try to understand." I replied irritably a moment later and thereby quenched his curiosity.

The auto-driver was young and therefore he could understand my agony and perhaps could even make use of my perfumes. The genuine desperation in my eyes touched his soul.

After a lot of thinking, he said, "These bottles look empty to me. I am not going to return more than 100 rupees."

The inherited bargaining skills from my mom came to my rescue at the right time. I bargained and bargained and at last the condition of *deal and no-deal* was finalized with Rs.120 being returned to me.

Having experienced the taste of triumph, I forged ahead in the searing sun. The sweat glands tried to play with my T-shirt but I resisted it by moving fast thereby conditioning my body against the wind. The wind was kissing my neck and it brought a strange tickle, which soothed my mood.

After about 20 minutes of wrestling with sweat, I reached the entry gate of the Central Secretariat Metro Station. With a sigh, I entered the place, which had a centralized AC *(to my delight!)*. My perspiration evaporated in no time and the *Axe* helped me with the other work. It was 11 am, and finally I was relieved that I would make it to the Kashmere Gate station, which was 20 minutes away, on time.

After all on any first date, it is *a MUST for any guy to reach on time*, otherwise the girl will keep taunting him about being late the entire life – and if she happens to come late, don't dare to point this out to her, because she'll thrash you with her reasoning power and make you feel guilty!

Happily I descended to the platform, with my former cool style back into action!

15
MS to PS!

11:02 am. As I proceeded towards the platform, a loud announcement was made, "There's an emergency. All the passengers on the platform are requested to come upstairs immediately!"

Several armed policemen, came to the platform through the lift. They had sniffer dogs and some super-fat costumed guys, who are popularly known as the *Bomb Squad*, accompanying them.

It did not take me long to realize that there was a bomb threat at the metro station. I wanted to rush out of the station as quickly as possible, since I did not want my special day to be remembered as my death day. I didn't tell Tanya about it, since I did not want her blood pressure to shoot up. When some fellow passengers and I reached near the metro station corridor, which was at a considerable distance from the platform, policemen came and surrounded us.

One officer commanded, "All of you; please assemble in the corridor. There's an emergency. Please be patient and cooperate with us in this critical situation. We will just check you thoroughly once and leave you. No need to panic!"

Another one ordered, "Switch off all your mobile phones and surrender them to us."

When asked why they were asking for mobile phones, they replied, "We don't want to attract media's attention to this place."

A policewoman came and collected all our mobiles. It brought great pain to give it up. All I wanted was to make just one call (rather just an SMS), but the policemen *(as well as policewomen)* have no feelings for such things.

With disdain, I switched off the phone. My special day had been *evil-eyed*. He played with me once again and this time He exploited *the terrorists* for ruining my day.

I blessed terrorists with all kinds of beautiful and creative abuses I could splutter out of my mouth.

Why do terrorists become active only during the weekends? Why not on weekdays, when I am burning my bottom in the lecture theatre of my institute!

These bomb threats always destroy my weekend plans since anytime such threats are telecasted on TV, my Mom bangs my Nokia Tune in its loudest pitch with a straight-forward advice, "*Beta, bahar mat nikalna, khatra hai.*"

To which I, despite being in the bomb prone area, would reply in a serene manner, "Don't worry Ma, I am in the campus, I won't go out."

How could I explain to her that her son likes to be a '*Khatron ka Khiladi*'?

Returning to the tough situation, it was already 11:20 am and to face the anger of one's newly made girlfriend on the very first meet was a scary thing in itself plus this bomb threat and security halts added bitterness to my terrible condition.

I had never been so frightened and irritated simultaneously. My *Khatron ka Khiladi* 'avatar' was buried in fear as I got to see some real 'khatra'.

The minute hand of my watch turned swiftly and soon the time drifted to 12' o clock. We all were literally caged for security checks. I was thinking about Tanya, predicting that she would be very angry with me. Our first official meet as a couple and I am not turning up! And even my mobile being switched off.

A sudden rush at the elevators made me realize that the squad was coming towards me.

12:15 pm. After they searched the entire metro station and found nothing - *that meant someone had played a prank with them* - they came to us to shower their rage of defeat upon us. All that I could see were metal detectors and sniffer dogs. It seemed as if the dogs outnumbered the policemen. I could feel that I was the one most in hurry amongst those two hundred passengers who had missed their train. I was desperate to pass the security checks as soon as I could and rush out to the Kashmere Gate Metro Station.

To impress the machine-gun carrying hosts, I began to set my hairstyle to give me a complete makeover from a cool-boy kind to an innocent geek. The policeman who came for the metal detector check smiled at me, perhaps to my Laloo Yadav hairstyle in contrast to the sexy outfit. I passed the metal detector test easily. Despite their keen efforts, the policemen were unable to detect any explosive chemical inside the Axe bottle.

Half an hour passed in the process of the metal detection test. Then was the turn of the sniffer dog. One policeman came along with a well-built Doberman towards me. I had never seen such a heavy built dog before in my life*(undoubtedly, it could be used as the brand ambassador of Pedigree)*.

Having already faced two dog bites in my childhood, I had and still have a great phobia of dogs, especially the healthy ones. As soon as I saw the man approaching towards me with THE dog, I started trembling in fear. The Doberman seeing my intimidated psyche attacked me, and sniffed the whole of my jeans. As it sniffed, my heart beat rose to its maximum frequency and I could almost hear its thumping.

Seeing a doubt in the policeman's attitude, I realized that there was another break for me for about two hours at least. The policeman's eyes clearly showed suspicion. Relying on that bitch*(sorry, dog!)*, he took me into his custody for interrogation.

Ironically, no other passengers were taken into police custody. My being in a great hurry gave Him another chance to mess with me. This time I had lost hope. This police thing is a strange issue; they don't mind detaining you for days even on a slight suspicion. Uncertain of what was in store for me; I became totally numb to the surroundings. With a gloomy face, I accompanied the policemen to their gypsy.

1.47 pm. I was seated in the rear seat of the gypsy with two policemen giving me interesting company and ironically, the same sniffer dog in the front seat. My heart was now somewhat controlled as I had been used to the dog for the last five minutes. Sitting in a police car can really make you feel powerful.

A bit fearful yet confident that my I-card of the institute would save me, I stepped out of the police gypsy. But alas, some things always screw up! *Ding Dong - I had left my wallet and my I-card was in my wallet.* I had no way to prove my identity to them on my own.

Entering the police station for the first time, it seemed to be a really cool experience. It was much the same as it is shown in the movies. A small lock-up room, constables seated at the door, old fans decorating the ceiling, yellow-tinged off-white walls, corners stained with betel spots, a dirty glass tumbler and a pair of handcuffs on the table.

One policeman asked me to park my butt on the stool and answer the questions being asked. They interrogated about my identity and I had no way to prove it. They don't go by words, neither by innocence of faces, they only go by fatal beatings and slangs. I related them my phobia for dogs and even showed them the scar of a dog-bite on my hand. But their attitude did not show any sign of the word called *'Convinced'*.

Their every question contained in itself a brand new slang. I was insulted to the max. Perhaps, that is the first degree they use to extract information out of suspicious people. I realized they are much more creative in the domain of slangs than I was, even they could compete with Aryan.

I had no option other than contacting my relatives, which I didn't want to do. The reason for that was my only relative in Delhi was my Uncle – who himself was the D.S.P of the South Delhi Police and the first thing he would ask would be why was I in the other part of Delhi all alone. The first thought that would strike his mind would be, *"Zaroor koi ladki ka chakkar hai!"*

I surrendered to the circumstances and finally called up my uncle. He talked to the policeman, rather fired them up. Within a minute, he faxed his identity-card and verbally confirmed my identity. After giving the necessary dose to the policeman, my uncle asked for me on the phone. Being a disciplinarian, he loved punishing innocent people like me for any small misdeed.

Uncle asked me, "What were you doing at the metro station? As far as I remember, you had said earlier that you had extra-classes during the weekend and therefore you didn't come to my house this weekend."

"Actually, Uncle, the class had been cancelled. I was just going to see a friend." I had to admit as my intelligent brain was too numb to invent any new lies that time.

Uncle disconnected the phone after a long "hmmmmmmmmmmm!"

This 'hmmm' is a strange word since it does not depict clearly whether it means a yes or a no, an annoyance or an indifference. But my uncle's last expression on the phone clearly showed his disgust at me. I just hoped that he would not convey this thing to my Mom!

When I hung up the phone, what I observed startled me. There was a sudden transformation in the policemen. They became an epitome of honesty and goodness. They started treating me like a maharaja, with coke and chips served on the table.

One of them said, "You should have told us earlier that you are DSP saheb's relative, we would not have bothered you."

How could I explain to them that all the while I had been fighting with this very dilemma - whether I should tell my uncle or not?

2.22 p.m. I asked them, "I need to rush as soon as possible."

The policeman handed back my stuff and set me free instantly. So finally, after all these trysts with errors, humiliations and finally elation, I was free. I came out of the police station and looked around. Never before had I appreciated silly things like fresh air, sun's warmth kissing my body and bird's chirping. With a blissful smile, I was enjoying the surroundings when it struck my mind – *It's still my special day.*

Within a moment, I switched my cell-phone on. There were 73 calls from Tanya that I had missed while my mobile was switched off. I had no idea how I was going to face her. Numerous thoughts were banging my head - *What would be in her mind? Will she still be waiting for me? Will she hear my explanations? And so on…*

Not only did the thoughts of her rage struck my mind, but also her beauty and love. Thoughts about her innocent smile and bashful laughter helped me forget about *the bomb and police ordeal* that I had just crossed over. I began to miss her even more and that brought even more frustration.

Feeling guilty, I prepared myself to face her anger and dared to call her. Full ring went on, but she rejected the call. I knew that she was angry.. I tried again and again for twenty seven times in a row. I could feel how angry she was with me!

God has gifted girls *(as well as women, no offense!)* in all aspects except one thing. That aspect is a very famous word called 'patience'. They are so good at getting impatient that we can even hold reality shows titled 'Miss Impatient' and make a channel climb up the TRPs. Their ear is allergic to hear any explanation – be it 100% genuine – even then; once they make an image of anything on their mental black-board *(that means girl can't imagine in colors!)*, that image gets imprinted almost permanently and could be modified only in very special cases!

It was my 28th attempt. I was determined to call her continuously until she picked up the phone. She finally gave up and received my call.

"Hello!" I gathered that much grit to stammer.

"I am not going to talk to you." She charged straightaway.

I replied serenely, "Please listen to me. I was..."

Before I could complete my sentence, she overtook me, "This is the height of everything, I have been waiting here in the metro station for the last three hours and you rascal didn't turn up! I hate you!"

Instead of feeling guilty, I felt elated. I was so astonished to hear that she was still waiting for me!

"She loves me with such a passion, Man you are very lucky!" I assured myself.

Her scolding echoed in my ears and I realized that *if I cried for mercy, I would not get it!* So the only way to make her listen was to stop her shouting.

Seizing the opportunity at the right moment, I increased my pitch to the maximum and screamed, "I was at the Police Station. Did you get that?" And then a full stop.

Instantaneously, her paradigm shifted and her new merciful avatar appeared; a welcome change from her previous *Chandalika incarnation.* She replied with concern, "What happened Kanav? Is everything all right?"

At last, it was *I who won*, for the first time though. I explained to her everything in lucid detail, except my empty wallet, of course.

"I am really sorry but I was helpless then. I had no other option other than obeying the policemen." I explained to her.

"I am very sorry for the outburst. Just forget about everything and come to the station. I promise that I will make this day special for both of us!" She replied bringing in a bucket of relief for me to bathe with for my entire lifetime.

I looked up and said, "Thank you God for giving me such an understanding soul-mate, but that does not mean that I am friends with you. I still can't forget how you messed up with me! We are still at war!"

For the first time in the whole day, there was no 'oops moment' that occurred. Everything was perfectly normal. I was back at ground level. Perhaps God had become tired; after all He also is a Man, indeed a very powerful Man, with quite special feelings for me this day!

16
A Twisted Beginning

2.49 pm I took an auto and went to the Central Secretariat Metro station. I entered the station, cautiously. The ambience of the station gave no hint of the condition two hours back. Time changed so swiftly. The security was tight, as I could see since the guard checked me quite cautiously this time. I went to the platform outracing everybody around me. It was obvious from my behaviour that I was really in a hurry.

The train took another five minutes to come. Till then, I stared at the camera at the platform fearlessly, which projected its circular mouth at me with a dangerous look. The sudden assurance of having a backup in the form of my uncle gave me the courage to do so.

The train arrived and broke my staring spell. The passengers made a great mess while boarding and deboarding the train simultaneously. Still, I managed to board the train and ran forward to capture the corner-most seat since it offered less encroachment from the standing passengers. I sighed and stretched my body to release the muscular tension.

The smell of Axe was lost in the last one hour long *hulchul* and I was too tired to open my bag again and spray it on me. I recalled earlier times when I used to board the metro just for fun.

Sitting on the seat, I recalled how I used to love boarding that very metro with Anuj quite a few times earlier just to have a glimpse of the glam-girls of Delhi and see Anuj's futile attempts to impress them. It seemed as if the whole **Page#3** of the Delhi Times were present in the compartment. This habit runs in the blood of all men, however naive they may seem, they always find a way to keep adoring the prettiest girl in the surroundings, stealthily.

Seeing an old lady standing in front of me, I offered my seat to her. She was very pleased with me and I too got lucky. I noticed later that my random act of kindness had impressed two beauties around. Two girls smiled at me simultaneously and I reciprocated being careful not to show my braces. After all, without my braces, I looked decently handsome! The first one was prettier and I kept looking at her from time to time without letting her notice.

"She is gorgeous!" I exclaimed in my thoughts.

"Oh! Wait a minute, what am I talking about! I am in love with someone and I am eyeing another girl. Isn't it unfair?" I questioned myself.

"This boyish tendency can't be conquered, since any attractive girl would still attract me" my sound logic solved my dilemma. Comprehending this complex philosophy I turned my eyes away from that girl, but it got fixed on another girl who was using an eyeliner on her eye.

I turned my head again, and *yeah, you guessed it right* - my eyes got stuck on another girl. Still, to remain as faithful as I could to my girlfriend Tanya, I began to look out of the window. Needless to say, the window also showed some reflections of interesting figures, which kept disturbing me.

The only difference in my attitude after getting committed was that this time *no-one* got into my crush list as earlier. My crush-list got its *'the-END'* with the advent of Tanya in my life. The glam-girls were more like the soft-drinks and Tanya was like water for me. No matter how many bottles of soft-drink you drink, your thirst gets quenched only by water!

3:10 pm The train reached the Kashmere Gate station. Coming back to my senses, I regained my excitement after facing such a rugged ordeal and weird glamour-olosophy. With just 100 rupees in my pocket *(Rs. 20 spent in the return journey after getting liberated from PS)*, I was going on my first official DATE. Funny isn't it?

I got out of train, looked around in the crowd. Three seconds later, a smiling face appeared out of nowhere and literally jumped on me. I got immensely shocked, never before had any girl hugged me, that too in public. Instead of enjoying the sensation, I became very conscious. While she was embracing me passionately, I was busy lowering my heartbeat to normal.

I was not even holding her, my hands were at my side. In the midst of about hundred people passing by, a quarter of who were staring at me, I was fighting with shock and uneasiness. I was uncomfortable by this sudden public display of affection showered upon me. The hug lasted for one and half minutes and my heartbeat came back to normal after a minute.

In the last thirty seconds, I put my arms around her and felt her. I could hear her deep gasps of breath on my shoulders and her silky hair kissing my palms. She did not say a word; she just surrendered herself in my arms. Her hair was very fragrant. I took a deep breath and closed my eyes to cut off the panoramic view of the platform.

"I missed you like hell for the last one month!" She bumbled after allowing her excitement to come to the ground level.

I opened my eyes; I was still there in her arms. The relative proportion of people staring at me increased, and again I became conscious of the passers-by.

I stammered, "Let us find a place to sit. We will talk at ease."

Being a beginner in the arena of love, I did not realize that my words could hamper the intensity of her emotions. Obviously, those were not the right choice of words, since I observed Tanya was not quite pleased to hear my reply. She left me, and moved a foot away. Any girlfriend would expect a romantic reply to her emotions, but not every boyfriend could be as stupid as me. I repented that I behaved callously when she was being truly herself.

As I can relate now, girls, I mean to say girlfriends, primarily want just one thing from a guy and it's their *sensitivity*. They should be sensitive enough to respond to their emotions coherently. But this funda of love was not clear to me that time, as I was a mere beginner, without even any sort of love-guru, in that field. I erred. But doesn't matter, since it's through errors that we learn!

A foot far from me, she stood. I glanced at her eyes but she looked away from mine. She was angry at me. I tried to touch her hand, but she moved it away and stood there unruffled.

She wore a T-shirt on which the quote was - *"ALL men are stupid and you are the King of them."*

Indeed those were the words telling the UNIVERSAL TRUTH aloud to me as well as to the world.

Trying to disprove my stupidity, I started, "When you have made me the King, then abide by my orders. Come along to McDonalds!"

She followed without saying a word. I made *a twisted beginning* to our first date; my creative mind was running out of ideas. I was just hoping for a miracle to repair everything but miracles take time to occur.

3:20 pm. We went to the McDonald's in the station premises itself.

Despite the noise of people chattering around, I could easily sense the silence between Tanya and me. There was no place in Mc Donald's, which was vacant.

Tanya and I, almost one foot apart, were standing near the door, hoping to get ourselves a seat. My thighs were hurting; all my stamina had been drained off in my adventure with errors throughout the morning.

Five minutes went by. Although two couples had finished their foodstuff, they were too lazy to lift their heavy butts up the chair and evacuate the seat. It took another five minutes to extinguish my desperation for a seat since one table, with just one chair, got free.

Seeing the chance, Tanya and I ran forward, outracing the other waiting customers, to capture that seat. Tanya turned out to be a good athlete, since she competed with me and in a moment we both jumped on the same chair simultaneously.

She pushed me aside and captured that chair. I toppled down, finally surrendering to *The Woman Power*. With a romantic rage, I glanced upon her face and she gave me a mischievous look with a growing smile.

"I win!" She exclaimed laughing at me with her focus becoming more and more intense at me. *I loved that look.*

For the first time in my life she was looking into my eyes so passionately. I instantly knew that the twisted beginning had been repaired and I had the full right to mess with her again! I extended my hand to her when she extended her right hand to pick me up.

It was all fun and romance around us, and I got an idea to multiply the fun ten times. Capturing her right hand, I pulled her back to me, made her fall on the floor and captured her seat.

She was looking at me as if she was going to eat me then and there.

Her expression became a cocktail of all the carnivores alive in Africa as well as Australia.

To tease her more, I shouted, "I win!" and winked at her. Finally, I extended both my hands towards her, while her expression still showed as if she was ready to attack me. I pulled her up, offered her my chair and borrowed a chair from the nearest neighbour who had been enjoying our *live-show*.

Laughter painted both our faces and the lull that had surrounded us for the last fifteen minutes vanished in a moment. For five minutes, we were literally playing *blink* and at last it was I who lost. As I blinked my eyes, two huge drops of tears rolled down my eyes. Perhaps those were the tears of love (*or due to the air friction!*), and they brought me goose-bumps.

I extended my hands to Tanya and she comforted them with the softest touch I had ever felt. She said very gently, "I love you madly."

Oh my God, these girls are gifted at saying the right thing at the right time. How could she know that I needed that phrase the most at that time? The ecstasy experienced can't be expressed here in words.

I was on *cloud nine* after hearing her endearing voice. If I am asked the best moment of my life I have ever had, then it was that moment. I had never felt so comforted, all my tensions and the weariness of the day were dissolved in the sea of love. It was sheer bliss.

"Where are you *bachcha*? Are you ok?" She said as she broke the chain of my thoughts.

"Yes, I was just thinking that God has blessed me by letting you enter my life. I am so very lucky!" I whispered as I gathered my senses back.

I tried to forget about the games that HE had played with me early in the morning. After all, *to forgive is divine! And to forgive the Divine is the most Divine!* As you can see, love really makes you a better person.

"Now let me make you luckier! As you won that chair game, I am going to give you a treat. Say, what do you want to eat?" She asked calmly.

That was a relief as I was too embarrassed to tell her about my belly-up condition. To please my opulent girlfriend as well as my appetite, I ordered the McD Combo Meal comprising every possible recipe to fill my starving abdomen.

As she went to the counter, I could not restrain my eyes from following her. She was looking gorgeous. I observed her carefully, with her T-shirt she wore blue jeans, much the same colour as mine, and her long silky hair hanging down her back, making her look like *an angel personified on Earth.* I became oblivious to the surroundings as I was lost in adoring her beauty.

She came back with the tray and I helped her at the table. She sat just in front of me, and I pierced her eyes with mine until she was abashed and turned them away.

"Where is the surprise you brought for me?" Tanya asked suddenly.

"You remember it? I thought you would forget it." I said.

"I don't forget surprises!" She replied.

"Ok. You will have to close your eyes for it." I said and she closed her eyes with a smile on her face.

"Here is your surprise. It's *we.*" I said and pulled out the ambigram having our names on it from both the sides.

"Wow, it's so beautiful. Have you made it?" Tanya exclaimed as she saw Tanya-Kanav.

"Yeah! Turn it 180 degrees and you will see the same thing once again." I said and turned the paper by 180 degrees. The names still embellished the paper.

"It's so artistic. You never told me that you knew how to draw one!"

"That's the surprise, isn't it?" I said. She took it and kept it in her wallet.

"You are such a sweetheart." Tanya said.

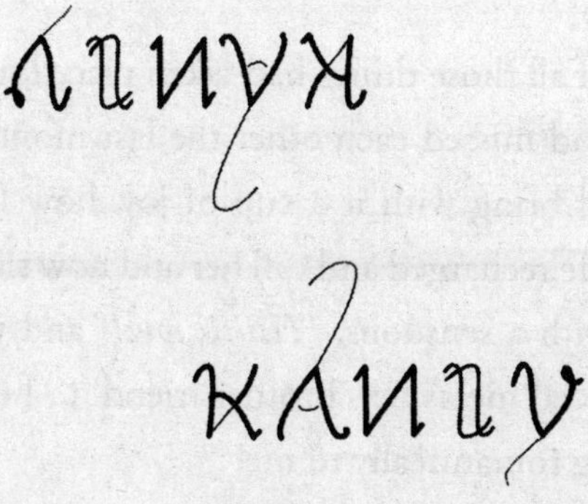

Some time later, the background song changed to the famous Titanic song - *'My heart will go on'* inducing romanticism in the surrounding and it gave me an invisible permit to flirt with her outrageously.

She started sipping her soft-drink grabbing the straw in her incisors fiercely, when I flirted, "Lucky the straw, I wish I had been at its place!"

Instantly, she took my hand and bit my index finger very hard. It hurt me – quite a lot.

"Do you still want to be in its place?" She said pointing to the straw with a nasty look on her face.

"Might be some other time." I said laughingly.

She showed her fist at me with a notorious smile. I gave her back a naughty look. I won back her heart and was prepared for the best *half-day* of my life waiting ahead of me. Optimism filled my mind and I was happy beyond imagination.

4 pm. Flirting continued for a while and then memories crept in. We began talking about our first meet, how formal we were, how she went away abruptly, how interestingly did I propose! She told me, "It was the most romantic yet the most unpredictable moment of my life!"

We talked as if all those things had taken place long ago! We talked about how we had missed each other the last month, how her every single call would bring with it a cup of joy, how I would stealthily getting my mobile recharged and call her and how she used to start off our every talk with a sensuous, *"Hiiiiii love!"* and just then she said how she introduced me as her 'brother friend' to her mom when she found her talking romantically to me!

Wait a minute, what did she say about me to her mom? A brother friend? What the hell was that?

"You insensitive jerk; you did not even think that I would never ever feel good about being introduced to your mom as your brother friend!" I yelled in shock.

"I know!" She said nodding her head horizontally.

"And why are you telling me about it now! Why didn't you tell me earlier?" I charged.

"I am sorry, but I thought I would tell you personally. Actually, as I had told you earlier, my mom is very strict about this love thing at our age. If she finds me hanging out with you, I will be me grounded for life. It does not matter whether you are good or bad, this love thing is an allergy to her. She regards love as mere rubbish, with always a bad ending!"

"This is ridiculous. How can love be having a good ending in her view when she herself is willing to give it a bad ending?" I questioned in an annoyed tone.

"We are both helpless. Leave it to time, her perception will change with it!"

"I hope so." I said with faint optimism.

"I would prefer listening to Himesh for my entire life than being your bro for life!" I humoured to annihilate the growing pressure.

"You don't need to punish your ear-drums for this silly thing. Don't you worry honey! I will transform you from Bro to Broom!" She chuckled.

"Broom????" I enquired with a puzzled look.

"Didn't you get that? Decode it? Let me see how much grey-matter you have got Mr. To-Be-Engineer!" She taunted me.

I knew that my grey matter was never enough to counter her weird mind. I resigned almost instantly.

"Poor you! It's the acronym I have invented instantly for Bridegroom: BRide-grOOM!" She explained and smiled with pride as if she would receive a Nobel Prize for it. *Aha! What a discovery? Broom…*

Girls are very productive at thinking rubbish *(Not ladies, mind it!)*. The rubbish that they think does not directly affect them but it does affect their boyfriends. Without even finding the statement funny, the guys have no choice other than to laugh and appreciate them. As every other ideal boyfriend, I did the same.

"Wow, you think so fast! You are so funny!" I flattered her completely.

I noticed that the curvature of her smile increased to nearly a semi-circle.

4.13 pm. Pleased, she held my hands tightly and assured, "Nothing can separate us. We are made for each other."

"Yeah, this Broom will always to Be your RIDE!" I used my so called engineering mind to create this sentence with BROOM and BRIDE together, plus, I indirectly meant that she needed to become *a witch* to use a broom-stick as her ride*(much like you see in Harry Potter!)*! But alas, she didn't notice the rhetoric.

Perhaps my thinking pattern was very complex for her mind to comprehend!

I did not try to crack any more jokes. I looked around while I noticed that she was looking into my eyes. I was observing her from my peripheral vision, and she kept her stare on. I was enjoying the moment, and after giving her two long minutes, I turned to her, when she suddenly drifted her vision away from me. *She was longing for me!*

A moment later,

"Let us find some quiet place." She said giving me a hint of what's coming ahead.

17
A Taste of Intimacy

4.20 pm. We came out of the metro station and wandered here and there, until we finally found a quiet place nearby. It was a rose garden. Other than some old ladies coming for their evening walk, there were very few couples present. The weather had taken a swift turn and was setting the mood for intimacy.

We walked through the fragrant muddy tracks crossing the gardens to the woods. We steered through the woods, talking about what that I also don't remember, to finally find us a small hillock nearby. Tall trees surrounded it and there was nobody around who could peep in, and even if somebody approached us then their footsteps would warn us beforehand.

The aroma of the surroundings seduced my heart and the sudden advent of clouds in the sky added colour to my emotions. Besides all that, it was Tanya's eyes that were drawing me towards them.

I dropped my bag down on one side of the hillock, and both of us climbed on top of it. I could feel it was the moment, *the first moment of intimacy* – might be the moment of *my first kiss*, depending on how Tanya responded.

Being a bit sweaty, I wanted to use my deodorant but I felt awkward to take it out in front of Tanya. Hoping the fragrance of the surrounding will dissolve my body-odour away, I prepared myself for what was going to happen. Excited, nervous and a little cautious, I tried to be as gentle as possible.

4.40 pm. It was just Tanya and me. I shifted nearer to Tanya and sat by her side putting my arms around her. She was behaving very shyly; her extrovert personality was transformed into a bashful young girl. She showed no resistance at all, she was ready for whatever I did. It seemed as if there was no one else on this planet other than the two of us.

As I approached nearer to her, she closed her eyes. I held her palms gently and pulled her towards me.

Just then, a loud sound saying, *"Hey wazzup?"* hit my ears.

Utterly shocked, I jumped off the hillock and fell to the ground. I got very scared thinking that someone might be noticing us. Lying on the ground, all I could hear was Tanya's voice. She was still on the hillock talking to someone. But the voice of that *someone* was not audible. Cautiously, I got up from the ground.

I was confused by what I saw - Tanya was on her phone. Seeing me, she giggled at my intimidated psyche and made me realize it was her ringtone that spoke up. It's embarrassing to be frightened in front of your newly-found girlfriend. Finding nothing extraordinary to counter her giggle, I showed my tongue at her to mock her.

While Tanya was busy talking on her phone, I seized the opportunity for some *ornamentation*. I pulled out the Axe from my bag. Don't get it wrong, Axe is the name of the deodorant I am talking about. I sprayed it all over my body especially the pulse-points *viz. wrists, the gap between lower lip and chin, hind-ears and pits!* Leaving no stones unturned, I took out my handkerchief and wiped off every possible drop of sweat on my forehead. Perhaps, this is what is called *preparation*!

Fully prepared, I was waiting for the call to be over. She was still on the phone when she signaled me to take something out of the right pocket of her jeans. While she was standing, I slid my index and the middle finger inside her right pocket and touched something strange, which I could not decipher despite my infinite wild guesses.

It was cylindrical, about two inches long and had a paper-like sheath around it with rough ends. To quench my curiosity, I tried to pull it out, but the friction offered by her ultra-tight jeans was too much to test the tensile strength of my fingers. Ultimately, I put my thumb inside her pocket and I pulled the thing out using the thumb and my index finger. After seeing the thing that I had pulled out, my face showed expressions worthy of a combination of both Jim Carrey and Govinda. The peculiar thing turned out to be the silliest thing I could think of. It was *Polo - the mint with a hole!*

Why should my girlfriend be lacking in her preparation, she was in fact much more prepared than I was! She was prepared for the subtle aspects of our date. You all being smart enough, I think I do not need to specify why she brought polo with her, but interestingly its particular use always requires the permission of the girl! Since men are always ready for it. *Haven't you seen Mika?*

5.05 pm. After being the best story-teller of the world for the last twenty minutes, Tanya came back to the present world - *the beautiful world with just the two of us!*

"Were you making amendments in the Constitution on the phone? Such a long talk!" I said as I switched on my satire mode.

"It was mom, enquiring about when I was to return. And you stop being sarcastic! "

"Sarcasm is the only service I can offer you for free." I said borrowing a T-shirt quote from a girl who I had seen at the metro station. I gave her the mint and dropped another one in my mouth.

"Very funny, your stolen one-liners can't impress me." She killed my pride in an instant.

"Anyway, what was she saying?"

"She would not be home in the evening since she has a kittie-party tonight at the Army Club. She asked me to reach by 7 o clock since our maid has to leave."

"Ok. By the way, you did a lot of preparation for today!" I said to her, pointing at the peppermint. She gave me a spicy look, which I took as the green signal to take the big step.

Within a moment, I approached her and captured her in my arms. I was so near that I could even count her breaths. She closed her eyes, and was ready for me to proceed. I held her in my arms and I bent my face towards hers. Just an inch away from her lips, my lips desperate to feel the warmth of hers, I closed my eyes to let me feel this sensation wholly. Before any sensation of touch pinched my nerves, something far more intense poked my ears.

"Aaaahchcheeeeeeeeeeeee!!!!!!" The intense sound slapped my ear-drums and about two million droplets comprising of her spit decorated my face in the most disorderly fashion. It seemed someone had done spray painting on my face with a colourless colour! I opened my eyes only to see her sneezing vehemently.

In the next two minutes, she sneezed thirty two times *(sixteen sneezes per minute can compete for a world record!)*. I just watched her from a distance wondering what had gone wrong!

After five minutes, this Sneezing Sensation came to a halt.

"God bless you – fifty eight times!" I exclaimed.

"Did you .... Aaahchcheeeeeeee....I mean did you count the number of sneezes?" She enquired.

"Yeah, God bless you for the fifty-ninth time!" I said and smiled.

"May I know the reason for this sudden tsunami of sneezes?" I enquired.

"It's you, duffer! Who told you to use musk deodorant? I am allergic to it!" She stated with another sneeze giving a full stop to the statement.

It's the problem you face if you propose to someone without even hanging out together for some time. How could you expect to know everything about someone you hardly spent some personal time with?

"I thought girls like strong deos! Nevertheless I had real fun counting your sneezes. You are just forty short of a century!" I humoured.

"Very funny, fetch me some water, otherwise I will continue Aaahcheeee!" She demanded.

Our quiet place didn't serve our purpose, and we had to go to a nearby market place to fetch some water for my sneezing stud.

A bottle of water was all it took for my *sneezing-maestro* to come to the normal level and meanwhile, I also washed my face to shrug off any sign of the scent. Still, she maintained a safe distance from me to avoid *the Axe-effect.* While walking through the market, we were desperate for a place to sit and chat.

5:30 pm. Amidst the hunt for some place to sit, a continuous faint chiming of bells in the background caught Tanya's attention. It gave her a clue that there was a temple nearby. I was too lost in my own self to notice that sound.

"I found a place for us to sit. Just follow me!" She led the way.

I had no idea where she was taking me, but as I approached the place, the intensity of the sound amplified and I realized that it was going to be my *encounter with HIM.*

Being a hard-core *anti-God element*, I was not quite in a mood to enter the place but I wanted to please Tanya after spoiling our last half-hour. I entered the place along with Tanya and she escorted me towards the idol of Lord Ganesha. The fragrance of flowers and the powerful atmosphere of the surroundings captivated me. We both sat in front of the idol and started chatting - for the first time a spiritual chat.

"God understands just one language and that's the language of love. Ask him anything with love and he will fulfill it." She said.

"You are such a *bhakta*. How come you know all this stuff?"I asked.

"I don't know how. I just do" She said while her eyes twinkled.

"Just close your eyes and ask anything you want" She ordered.

"Hmmm."

I closed my eyes. After getting bored in just five seconds of meditation, I opened my eyes and glanced at her. Her eyes were closed in prayers. Her face was shining with a slight smile that seemed as if God was answering her prayers. Forgetting my prayers, I was lost in her - adoring her innocence. She looked beautiful - as always - and love was the only language that I could understand at that moment. My unasked prayers had been answered in the form of Tanya.

Seeing nobody around I moved ahead and kissed her cheek and instantly went back to my original position with my eyes closed like a yogi. The ten long seconds of my novice meditation got its break when something happened. A soft touch on my cheek brought a 'The End' to my long concentration spell.

Goosebumps, goose-bumps and goose-bumps erupted all over my body along with a swooping sensation in my stomach. I opened my eyes and I found the two most beautiful eyes of the world right in front of me. They were looking at me with tears lining the lashes.

"What happened honey? Why are you crying?" I asked.

"I love you." It was all she said.

"Is that the reason? Am I so bad?" I chuckled.

"Shut up you duffer!" She said laughingly. More tears dropped down her eyes as she laughed.

"C'mon tell me, what did you pray for?" She asked.

"I could not pray, you disturbed me while I was praying" I said pointing to my cheek.

"I disturbed? You are saying as if you didn't do anything?" She scolded.

"When I closed my eyes, all I could see was you. Even God became invisible in your radiance."

"Enough of flattery. Don't bring God into all this!"

"Yeah He is so innocent! You seem to be his die-hard fan. Now I realize why opposites attract!" I stated sarcastically.

"By the way what did you ask Him?" I enquired.

"I won't tell!" She said with an attitude.

There is a time when the girl is in an ultra-good mood, and that mood has a special gift for the guy. It is a test of his patience. Girls know that ultimately they will have to tell the thing, but they just love teasing *'their-guys'* to make them more and more curious. Thankfully, the pathetic Internet speed of the hostel had endowed me with patience in abundance.

"Please tell na honey! Please..." I knelt before her and said.

"No..." She said with her attitude climbing the charts.

"Please..." I pleaded as I prostrated in front of her with my hands joined as if in prayers. The people around me in the temple were having a good laugh at my action. Tanya was embarrassed to the max and she cried to me to stop my buffoonery.

One of the persons from the crowd commented, "*Bhagvan idhar nahin udhar hai.*"

"*Pehle insaan ko to mana lu, fir bhagvan ko manaunga*!" For the first time in my life, I felt my wit working.

Tanya, being very frustrated with me, pulled me up and took me out of the temple-premises.

"Please tell me now, otherwise I would kneel down on the road!" I warned her to make her feel that I was truly desperate to know what she prayed.

"I prayed for our togetherness forever." She replied with a smile finally giving me respite from my listlessness.

At last, I won. Though I was a tyro in the field of girls, I was learning quite fast. I had passed the real test of my patience and withstood Tanya's fuss with insurmountable tolerance. Deciphering the psychology of a girl is the most difficult task in this universe and I was glad to realize that I was quite skilled at it.

I smiled back at her. A minute later, we came out of the temple and proceeded on our way when I noticed a florist shop outside the temple.

"Please wait here. I am just coming." I asked Tanya and ran forward to the shop. I purchased a red rose for her, worth 20 bucks *(now, I had only 80 rupees balance)* and hid it in my bag.

I rushed back to Tanya when she asked, "What happened?"

"Nothing just went to see something."

"So am I getting a red rose?" She knew my intention.

"A red rose for what? There are better ways to do an extravaganza than buying you a red rose." I poked her.

18 The Summer Rain

5:50 pm. We forged ahead, talking about 'us' all through the way. She forgot about that rose on the way, though she might have been expecting that I would sooner or later present it to her.

Along the road, the weather was playing ping pong and it became quite unpredictable. The clouds darkened and the whole surrounding became dark at 6 o clock only. The scorching heat during the day was now to be vanquished with the advent of rains. A bit dark and quixotic, the air carried a special aroma of the ground and rain mixed together. Winds pervaded the road, and we thought of getting to a shelter from the dust-storm for the time being.

We stood on the edge of the road protecting our eyes from the dust-storm with our hand. We were waiting for an auto. Seeing an auto, Tanya waved to it. It stopped in front of us. As she went towards it, she waved me a bye and that was when I seized the moment. I caught her hand from the bye position and dragged her towards me and gave her a tight hug.

The auto-wala was relishing the sight in front of him, though the darkness could not offer him much clarity. I kissed Tanya's cheek, and said, "I love you".

"I love you too. Will call you at night!" She said in her most romantic tone.

'I love you' is such a beautiful phrase, no matter how many times you repeat it; you could never ever get bored of it. There are no other phrases so used, so clichéd yet so beautiful in the English Language.

I released her and looked into her eyes. With her eyes affixed on me, she secured her place in the auto and shouted, "Take care. Thank you for giving me the best day of my life."

I smiled and waved back. I was so lost in her ecstasy that I even forgot to gift the red rose that I had bought for her.

6:12 pm. As she asked the auto-wala to go, I felt a drop of rain falling on my face. Hurriedly, I screamed "Tanya" at my loudest pitch. The auto stopped about ten meters ahead. Tanya was looking back with just her head popping out of the auto.

"What happened, you scared me!" She said, shocked.

I went to her and wiped the drops of rain, which had just fallen on her face, and said, "It's raining. I can't leave you alone. It isn't safe. I am accompanying you to your place."

"You don't worry, I can go alone. If my mom sees you then she will kill you."

"I don't mind losing my life to my to-be-mother-in-law. It is not safe to go alone in this weather." I said and pushed her inside and sat next to her. I asked the auto-wala to drive ahead.

"You are crazy man! Promise me that you are not going to step outside the auto there!" She said.

"I promise I won't!" I assured her.

"I won't ever cause any trouble to you." I whispered.

"You are going to cause the biggest trouble to me. I will have to convince my mom for your transformation from Bro to Broom.

Remember?" She defeated me with her counter logic.

Rains had taken a swift turn towards turbulence. Wind started blowing very riotously and it hit the windscreen of the auto hard. The auto had to exert quite a lot of force to travel ahead. There are some times in an engineer's life when you can't help noticing Newton's laws playing in front of you.

I pulled the side covers of the auto to provide a restriction to the rains to creep in obliquely. All these things were not disturbing me at all, since the darkness offered me an opportunity for intimacy. I held Tanya's hand tightly. An extremely shrill thunder scared Tanya and she apparently jumped over me and held me very tight.

"Thanks for accompanying me." She whispered and suddenly gifted me a kiss on my cheek. *I love surprises!*

I put my arms around her and kissed her forehead. The rain outside became more and more fierce and a left turn on the road, I didn't know how, helped the stream of rain water to travel along the edges to a hole on the side of the auto's covers to bump straight into our heads.

Neither of us wanted two baths in a single day, so I asked the auto-wala to stop the auto on finding any proper shelter. After exploring every possible place for shelter for the next five minutes, he finally stopped the auto at an old dilapidated bus-stop, which was completely isolated.

We got off the auto and instead of waiting for me to come along, Tanya ran forward towards the bus-stop seeking shade. That indirectly meant I had to pay the auto-driver. It would not have mattered to me had I been carrying a full wallet, but my belly was up and so I got a little perplexed.

Unwillingly though, since my girlfriend was unconcerned seeing me getting drenched in the rain, I paid the auto-wala his share of my wallet - 50 bucks*(now just 30 bucks were left in my pocket).*

Tanya was busy drying her hair with her small handkerchief, when I climbed the small step of the bus stand and stood just next to her. I gave her my handkerchief – the third one – it indeed came into use, as expected. I loved the sight - her long hair temptingly wet - looking as if she had just come out after her bath.

I was lost in adoring her when she broke the minute-long lull.

"What? What are you staring at?" She asked.

"I am staring at the girl who seems to have taken bath after a century." I taunted.

"You are so mean!" She said. The mischievous look on her face assured me that she was not serious and therefore I carried on my frequent *taunts-n-tease.*

6.40 pm. Rain was not in a mood to take a break and therefore, I asked Tanya to SMS her mom that she was caught in the rain, so that she doesn't worry. Tanya did so and she began inspecting the place. Though the rain did not offer much clarity of vision, she realized that this place was quite near to her home.

Her mom replied to the SMS, "I am going to leave at 7. You return as soon as you can," thus providing us, especially me, a sudden joy since I realized that we had got some more time to spend together.

Vehicles were plying on the road despite the heavy rains at a frequent rate. A car crossed the road quite close to us and sprayed the dirty water on the road upon us. *God only knows why those people play NASCAR on roads during heavy rains.*

I opened the bag to take out a handkerchief out of my secured set of handkerchiefs to wipe off the dirt, when I observed that forgotten red rose. I closed the zip of my bag again, not completely though, and through a small opening in the zip, I slid down my hands inside the bag and caught hold of the rose by its stem.

"I haven't proposed to you till now officially. Let me seize the moment. We won't get a more romantic time for it than now." I said looking into her eyes with full emotions.

"So you did the extravaganza at that florist shop. I knew it!" She said with excitement.

I nodded and knelt down in front of her and said, "It may seem simple, nothing unique and clichéd but it means so much to me – I just want to tell you that I love you madly Tanya. Will you be my love for life?" I was looking into her eyes.

Initially as I proposed, she was overwhelmed, with her eyes nearly wet, and whispered a clear *'yes'* but the moment I pulled my hands from the bag, she burst into the most demonic laughter I had ever seen.

I could not get what the cause of her laughter was until I saw what I held in hand. It was just the stem of the rose. The rose got stuck in the zip, dislodged itself from the stem and fell back into the bag. The only thing that came out was the stem and it was what I was proposing Tanya with. *Poor me!*

Embarrassed, I stood up and I stood there perplexed. Suddenly, I found a perfect way to bring an imperfect end to her demonic laughter. In an instant, I went ahead and sealed my lips with hers. It lasted just for about four to five seconds, and it felt *awesome.* Lips were wet due to the rain, with her lips warmer than mine - it felt as if someone was massaging my lips with a lukewarm wet-cotton ball. Her breath intermingled with mine and without even polo in our mouths; it tasted very cool and sweet.

She was stunned by what happened, stunned positively to emphasize.

Her eyes expressed all the thoughts she had and it seemed that there were no boundaries between us. I just did it on an instantaneous instinct without even preparing anything before that. 'The first kiss' as it seemed to be quite a big thing, turned out to be short and sweet for us.

Earlier I had daydreamt about this first kiss so many times, how would it feel, how would I initiate this kissing and there it happened just in a click of time. My first kiss turned out interesting in a very unique way, since both of us experienced exaltation. Our new experience provoked us to do it once again.

7.10 pm. We did not speak for the next two minutes, being lost in the ecstasy. The problem with the first kiss is that it makes you want more and more. The interesting thing is that it's not only a case with guys only but girls also enjoy it *(secretly!)*.

Suddenly, I moved my face ahead to kiss Tanya again when she turned her face sideways.

"Kanav, behave. It's a public place. Find a secluded place first." She chided me.

"You suddenly started talking sense." I complimented her.

"One should have a level-head. Isn't it?"

"Hmm, one should but it's not a MUST!" I teased her.

Time passed by and the rain somehow appeared to disappear, though the thunder was still on. As the violent rain transformed itself into a soft drizzle, we proceeded towards her home, strolling as slowly as we could. I noticed that there was a sudden change in my attitude; I became very desperate to find some place around us that was hidden from the passers-by to allow us to capitalize on our new kissing experience.

But alas, at seven in the evening, no matter how dark the surroundings are, you can't find a place free from the intense lights of the parabolic reflectors of the vehicles.

7.20 pm. Unsuccessful in my efforts to find a place, we reached the corner leading to Tanya's home. I realized that my wonderful day was going to end. But, there was a surprise waiting for me. Before I could see her off; she took charge and said –

"Here is a surprise for you: Mom might have left for her Kittie by now. Stay here for sometime as I go and check whether she has left or not. I will call you if she is not there otherwise I will give you a *misser.*"

She too wanted some more intimacy after the warmth of our first kiss.

"Ok." I bumbled.

"You know what to do then?" She asked.

"Yeah I suppose. I have to come to your place if you give me a *misser* and go home if you happen to call me." I poked her.

After thinking for twenty seconds she realized what I said.

"I hate you!" She said laughingly as she gave me a *milli-second* long hug and went away to disappear inside the main gate of her house.

Nervous of what was coming ahead, I was desperately hoping that she would give me a full ring. I looked around the place; there was just one street-light dimly lighting the anterior as well as the posterior end of the road with some cars parked along the houses. My keen eyes moved hither and thither to finally notice that there was an ice-cream booth situated almost opposite to Tanya's duplex.

19
The best time of my life

7.25 pm. A sudden tickle in my legs tripled my heartbeat. I instantly pulled out my cellphone from my pocket. It rang twice and got cut. To my disappointment, I realized that it marked the end of my special day. A missed call meant that her mom was at the home. My mind was not ready to accept such an abrupt ending to my beautiful day. After half a minute of contemplation on nothing in particular, I started my journey back to hostel and dragged myself towards the main road. A sudden realization of how tired I was crept into my mind, and I started feeling very weary.

7.28 pm. I had barely walked a hundred steps when my phone rang again. I was feeling so down that I didn't pick it up at the first instant. Then as it continued ringing, I pulled it out lazily to be shocked seeing Tanya on the phone.

I picked up the phone, "Your mom isn't there? Then that missed call?"

She took charge, "I made you a *BAKRA*. You were returning, isn't it?" She had a heavy doze of laughter fabricating a mockery-tail to her statement.

"It was not at all funny. I hate you more than anyone in this world" I said after being really pissed off with her bizarre prank-sense.

The disappointment was whitewashed with excitement again and the weariness was vanquished by the sudden happiness in anticipation of what was awaiting me at her place.

As I went ahead, I bought two butterscotch ice-cream cones from the booth to provide both of us with a tasteful experience, emptying my wallet completely. I opened the gate to her campus, proceeded to her house holding the two cones in my hand, only to find that the pad-board of her main door was locked from outside.

Wondering, I turned around towards the main gate, only to find the most gorgeous girl of the universe standing there and smiling at me. She had changed from her T-shirt into a simple white top and she was looking a hundred times more attractive in it. She smelt wonderful with her fragrant perfume doing a sleek task of seducing the geek within me.

"You go to the garage, I am coming in two minutes" She said, pointing in the direction of the garage as she went inside her home.

"Hmmm." I said even forgetting to offer her the ice-cream in my hands.

Fortunately, the cones had not yet started melting. I was tempted to start eating mine but my *'boyfriendish attitude'* restrained me. I didn't question her decision of choosing the garage as a place for *'our first make out'* because it was her place and she knew what was perfect for us! I moved to the empty garage, which was abnormally dark.

The garage was actually a car shed, with asbestos providing the roof for the three-sided cubicle. The smell of the rains was still in the air and the atmosphere was a bit cold. With strange darkness pervading the garage, all I could see with my eyes wide open was a white wall ornamented with speckles of grease on it. There were two dark speckles of grease resembling closely *two coherent eyes*. To my horror, they were staring at me. The very sight was dreadful.

The realization - I was going to make love in front of these devilish eyes - provoked a bizarre laugh in me, when suddenly someone touched my shoulders from behind. Horrified, I jumped and ran towards the main gate being conscious not to drop the ice-creams. Catching my breath, when I stopped at the gate, all I could hear was a familiar laugh coming from inside the garage. Tanya came out of the garage laughing her head off and stared at me with her eyes full of mischief.

7.45 pm. I once again had become *an object of ridicule* in front of her. Embarrassed, I went ahead in super-short steps towards her.

"You are such a child!" She said, with the most beautiful smile of the world on her face.

I had nothing to reply to her compliment, so I just shrugged my shoulders - in a way saying - *'I know'.*

"How could you reach here when that front door is closed?"

"There is a back door buddy. I have locked the front door from inside so that if somebody comes I will run inside through the back door and greet him or her. You can then secretly get out of the house whenever you get a chance. Until then hide yourself in the garage!"

"What if your mom comes? I mean if a car comes to the garage?"

"I suppose mom is not going to come till 9. And moreover, I am not gonna entertain you for more than ten minutes. Even if a car comes towards the garage, you hide yourself near the back door and move out as soon as possible."

"And mind it, we are having nothing more than a smooch!" She ordered with conviction.

"So you liked the kiss at the bus stop. I got you!" I took charge from her mockingly.

"Very funny!" She said dismissing my mockery in an instant. She repeated that phrase for the fifth time in the day.

"Kanav, I am serious. Nothing more than a smooch!" She exclaimed.

After contemplating for a long time, "As you wish!" I said hiding my slight disappointment.

I had to be nice; I did not want to lose the single opportunity I had got, by being driven by lust. To add to the irony, I was not really disappointed. I too didn't really want to go too fast. I liked it step-by-step. So a passionate long smooch would perfectly give a happy ending to my date. The garage thing was risky too since her mom did not have a fixed time to return home, so I wanted to be as swift as possible.

"Good. Now would you mind giving me the ice-cream before it melts completely?" She demanded.

"Oh! Yeah sure, I almost forgot about it." I giggled.

"You need to pay me for this, I am totally bankrupt now" I stated the truth seeing her cool mood and I handed over the cone. She accepted the half-melted cone happily and relished it.

"Mr.Bankrupt! You had a date without even sufficient money? You are really impossible."

"You don't need to carry money if your girlfriend is rich!" I teased her.

"Very funny! By the way, how much money do you need?" She buried my humour completely. She was gifted at this task.

"Just about 200 bucks. Don't bother now. Give me after some time." said.

"Some time, hmmm?" She inquired with a cunning smile.

"Some time as in the time taken to finish the ice-cream. Stop twisting our dirty mind!" I got an edge over her.

The next few moments, we both started concentrating on our ice-ream more than on ourselves.

Butterscotch being my favorite, I ate faster and assimilated the whole of the cone in no time while she was still struggling with the upper half of the scoop.

Having nothing extraordinary to do than watching her eating, I decided to add some fun. I pushed her right elbow up which painted whole of her face - especially her lower lip and chin - with the ice-cream. She was looking like a cat with her eyes shining in darkness.

"I am really sorry!" I tried to be genuinely sorry but couldn't resist my smile.

"You are so stupid." She said in an irritated tone.

"And you are making me a Cupid. Let me help you!" I said. The moment I had been waiting for, had finally arrived.

My heartbeat rose as I moved ahead to lap up the sprinkled butterscotch on her face with my tongue. I was nervous, my mind was quite anxious in taking this leap into intimacy. But nothing can stop the desire of love. With both my lips on her chin, I created a kind of suction mechanism and cleansed her cream painted face. I made sure that I don't leave any trace of butterscotch - my favorite flavour.

"Your some time is over, isn't it?" She taunted.

"No, it has just started!" I replied and I took the cone from her.

With the cone in my hands, feeling like *'Da Vinci - the Junior'*, painted the whole area circumscribing her lips with the melted butterscotch and moved near her. As I went ahead, she closed her eyes. I threw the incomplete cone of her ice-cream on the ground because now there were things that were yummier than the ice-cream.

Her eyes were closed in anticipation of my proximity. I could hear her breaths - they were deep and sensuous. Just that moment, the mischief king inside me woke up from its deep slumber. I had a tough decision to make - I had to choose between lust and mischief - and interestingly, I chose mischief. *Between two evils, I chose the one which I had never tried before.*

Instead of giving her a long passionate kiss, I moved near her ears and gusted air from my mouth at the maximum possible velocity. Her ear-drums might have become numb for a minute and she opened her eyes only to find me laughing at her. I took revenge for all the mockery she had subjected to me throughout the day.

She was furious and finding nothing unique to counter the mockery, she jumped on me and kissed, kissed and kissed. In a way, she borrowed the idea invented by me at the bus stop.

I closed my eyes to feel the sensation with much more clarity. It was long, passionate and rejuvenating. Not only that, it was delicious too - the flavour of butterscotch and the aroma of her perfume made me feel in heaven. The kiss lasted for about two minutes until we both started gasping for breath.

The garage with its exceptional darkness provided me a great opportunity for proximity with my soul-mate. With nothing more than a few mosquitoes to disrupt the harmony, I hugged her tightly and said, *"You are my life, And my to-be wife."*

"See, your love made a poet out of me." I continued.

"Yeah a silly poet out of you!" She mocked.

She came near me and seemed as if she was going to kiss my cheek. Not much later, I found that she was approaching my right ear.

"You are the favorite mistake of my life." She whispered as she came close to me. I liked the phrase - *'the favorite mistake'.*

"Don't make any more mistakes buddy!" I scolded her laughingly.

Just then, she bit my ear. I got goose-bumps, yet again.

I just had my second kiss - the most romantic one of my life till then – a life with the experience of just two kisses! I knew it was just a start – rather a pleasant start. That kiss was very special to me because it was Tanya who initiated it. If I could stop time, I would have stopped it the moment she jumped on me.

The second smooch enticed us more and we wanted another one to continue our show but Tanya had some different plans in her mind.

"This is going to be the last one!" Tanya stated with 100% seriousness.

"Please, not the last one!" I pleaded.

"Yes, it is!" She was unmoved.

"Let us make a deal. The person who first removes the lips loses. If you lose you will have to give me another kiss else it would be the last kiss." I made my condition clear. It meant either way it would turn out to be the longest kiss of my life.

"If I win, then you wouldn't bug me for more!" She ordered.

"I promise, I won't!" I pleased her.

"Ready for the last one?" She implied some pro-competition tactics.

"Yeah, ready for the second-last one." I missed no opportunity of pulling her leg.

20
OOPS!

A deep breath taken and once again we started our mutual task with more passion. For the third time in my life, and a second time in succession, a sensuous kiss again. I felt the old saying - time passes slowly when you make love – come true in front of our eyes. None of us wanted to finish first, as we had a deal earlier.

I tried to have my eyes wide open to see into Tanya's eyes while we kissed. I just wanted to see her feelings reflected through her eyes.

In almost complete darkness, I tried to see into her eyes, only to realize that they were closed. I turned my eyes towards the wall where the two haunting speckles looked directly into my eyes. With my third kiss still on, I twisted my head by a right angle to the other side to avoid my encounter with those appalling eyes.

After a two minutes long smooch, lust popped up in me and made me unconsciously move my right hand inside Tanya's shirt from the back. The touch of my cold hand on her back made her shudder with goose-bumps all across her body and a sudden current passed through her body giving her a short tremble.

Much like any other ideal girl, she too *'tried'* to move away from me, but unfortunately she couldn't. It was not because of the deal she was going to lose if she moved away, since giving one more kiss would not cost her much; but it was something else – something worth giving attention to.

It was neither her nor me single-handedly, that was stopping her, but it was our joint effort that made the effect. In fact, her upper lip was clumsily snarled up in my teeth - specifically in my braces.

She tried to move away once again only to be inflicted with more pain on her lip. She groaned an indistinct *'Ouch!'* that was more like *'Awwww!'* as I tried to detach my braces from her lip.

I was wondering how this entanglement could take place on its own. After thinking for about two minutes, all I could decipher was that it was my own action that was its root cause. I realized that my twisting and turning through a right angle while the third kiss was still on had bruised her inner lip and a small part of the bruised lip had got entangled in my braces.

If I moved any further then she would experience the force and thereby immense pain in her lip. If either of us tried to dislodge this entanglement from its place, she would be the one who will be hurt, as we couldn't decipher the way her lip was trapped. I had no choice at all because every possible idea seemed to end up developing a septic-infection in her inner lip.

We were both standing, with me bending down a little to reach the same level as Tanya. If a third person saw us at that instant, one might think that a hunchback was busy kissing a girl.

We could not even speak properly as our mouth was blocked. I tried to do a roll back action i.e. I twisted and turned my face exactly in the opposite way that I had done before. I curved the right angle anti-clockwise, trying to unhook her lip from my braces but things got worse. It brought more entanglement and more complication.

The situation reminded me of the deal we made before kissing and brought a strange laugh in me – seeing that none of us was going to take his/her lips away for quite sometime.

It might be worthy to bring to notice that my third kiss could make it to the Guinness Book for the longest kiss in the world. I held Tanya close in a way reminding her not to worry since I was there with her, but ironically it was my presence that was the source of her worry.

Exhausted after numerous tries, I decided to relax for some time. Having nothing extraordinary to do, I began looking at the speckles on the wall - the same speckle that made me an object of ridicule.

I could relate a familiarity in its shape since it reminded me of someone - someone who had been sleeping for a while with His attention distracted elsewhere. I unconsciously got an intuition saying that 'He is back'. A sudden fear of being caught started entrapping my mind. Two minutes later, my fear turned into reality.

8.10 pm. A sudden noise at the gate made both of us scared as hell. HE was definitely back - back with a BANG! The sound of the gate doubled our pulses and we could hear each other's heartbeats. The feeling of being close was dissolved in the fear of being caught. We tried to look at the gate at the same time but our messed up situation didn't allow us to do it together. I just hoped that no-one was coming towards the garage.

I gave Tanya the golden opportunity to observe who was at the gate. To facilitate her, I turned back with my eyes confronting the wall and Tanya's body hidden behind mine with her eyes seeing the gate through my shoulders. Her lip was still intertwined in my braces. She started trembling as soon as she looked at the gate.

Perplexed for a moment, I held her more tightly in my arms thereby providing her stability. Her trembling frequency doubled almost every other second. I held her tight with my hunchback mode still on and tried to decipher the reflection at the gate through her eyes. All I could see was darkness.

I was too much involved in Tanya. Her trembling body and more-than-audible heart-thumping made so much noise that I did not even get to notice the sound of the car that was entering the campus through the main gate.

It was only when an intense bright light steered through the darkness making a shadow of just the two of us on the back wall that I felt the tragedy of the situation. The two speckles which had played with me for the last fifteen minutes vanished in the darkness of our shadow.

As I see now *(yes, I am still alive!)*, I learnt a great lesson of human psychology that time - Sometimes even light, rather than only darkness, can scare the hell out of you. *But when light does so, it means you are doing something wrong – something terribly wrong!*

8.15 pm. "Mo…m!" Tanya spoke in broken tone, as if her voice was being shaken using a mixer-grinder. I was flabbergasted – I was going to encounter the person I feared the most. It was Tanya's mom in the car, coming to park the car in the garage. Tanya's eyes were horrified seeing her and I had no option other than having 'my back' welcome her with unopened arms. The car stopped about 10 yards away and its door opened. I could hear sounds of rapid footsteps directed towards us. We were caught red-handed in a position which no mother could withstand seeing her daughter in.

Sometimes, there comes a moment in your life when you desperately wish that all the atomic bombs, dynamites and explosives explode at the same time leaving you not even an infinitesimal chance to exist. I wanted to scream the biggest *'oops'* of my life but my hooked up teeth made even that impossible for me.

Tanya was shaking like a drunken monkey and to provide her extra-stability, I held her very cautiously while her mother approached us. Tanya's mom came to our side and surprisingly burst on Tanya first. She pulled Tanya by her hair and as expected; my face too got dragged along with her.

She couldn't notice that her lip was hooked up in my braces and all that she did was - she remained shocked at my obstinacy. She slapped hard at my face only to notice that Tanya's face also moved along with mine.

Tanya was trembling vigorously all throughout the time and I realized that I had to carry out the tough task of explaining our condition to Tanya's mom. In my snarled up situation, I dared to ask her help.

"Please hold her!" I asked her in my indistinct voice.

Perhaps she could only hear the phrase 'hold her' clearly as only saying that phrase didn't require the use of my messed up teeth and lips. She might have thought I was ordering her, as her shocked eyes told me. *Interestingly, she abided by my request, don't know why!* She must have realized by then that I was not quite an obstinate dog running wild after her daughter, rather was a kind of caring guy.

She saw the cumbersome position we were into and taking the situation quite maturely, she moved forward to get ourselves out of this messy situation.

I felt that Tanya's mom was a nice lady. I mean she agreed to help us out, which can be appropriately taken as her credential for being *nice!* I hoped that she forgave the two of us for our heinous act *(though the act was not at all heinous for us, rather it felt wonderful!)*

But, Tanya's non-stop sobbing and tremble stabbed my on-growing hope. After all, *my Tanya* wouldn't be trembling in fear seeing her mom, *if her mom were too lenient!*

Tanya, seeing all that, was stunned and her tremble vanished in the unexpected help her mother bestowed upon us. Tanya was nevertheless busy, crying her heart out. I felt pity for her.

'She might get a huge thrashing at her home - maybe she is grounded for days - God knows what will happen.' I thought.

The tears flowed through her eyes and through her upper lip it reached my mouth too. It was saline, much like brine served with a pinch of atmospheric dust. However, I swallowed it considering this could turn out to be my last memory of Tanya.

Tanya's Mom took us, careful not to hurt any of us, in front of her car's bright headlights to get a clear view of the entanglement, while my eyes that were facing the headlights were dazzled. I closed my eyes only to open it some time later after hearing Tanya's loud cry, *"Ah!"* when her Mom tried to detached her lip from my braces.

After about three minutes of concentrated efforts, her Mom was successful in extricating her lip from my braces safely. Tanya finding herself free; cried out loudly and ran through the back door inside her home leaving me alone to face the epitome of rage and furore all on my own.

I recalled the deal, which we had before the third kiss and actualized that I had won it since Tanya was the one who ran away from our entanglement. Although being a winner, I did not feel like one...since my second-last kiss had been pushed to the last kiss. Indeed, I managed to have it as *the longest kiss* in the world history.

Happy, shouldn't I be after experiencing the taste of triumph! *Alas, sometimes even the trophy of triumph contains explosives!* Even a Chief Guest was present especially to give me the trophy. The award ceremony was just going to start and I was waiting, being prepared for slaps, humiliation and what-not! The seemingly *nice* lady was now ready to unmask her real face.

8:30 pm. It was just her mom and I in the garage with the headlight making our shadows on the back wall. I could hear Tanya's faintly audible sound coming through the back door. She sounded sexy even while wailing.

I was standing in front of the danger; my fear had been vanquished by remorse. Remorse of not what happened but rather the remorse of being caught red-handed. She was the one who would have to transform me from *bro-to-broom* one day but considering what the situation was I just wished that she would let me return safely to my hostel-room. I lowered my eyes making her feel that I was guilty, which I definitely was, to an extent. I expected a hard slap, a severe thrashing and I was waiting for all my expectations to come true, but alas, it didn't.

Tanya's mom was staring at me intently. Tired of boredom seeing the same pair of dreadful eyes for about a minute, I began moving my eyes to and fro over the ground to pass my time. It seemed as if I was trying to decode the composition of molecules that constituted the ground.

The headlights of the car were still on. My vision drifted here and there and finally it became glued to our shadows on the back wall and found out that I was quite a bit taller than her - *she must have been relieved seeing that the person her daughter was seeing was not a hunchback!*

I checked my sudden smile which popped out of the above realization and I felt how critical my situation was, considering me standing in front of someone more dreadful than even the terrorists of Al-Quaeda.

After a score of oscillations of my eyeballs, I raised my lowered head a little only to notice that her gaze was still on. Tanya left me alone in front of an inevitable danger, whose eyes seemed more horrifying than those grease spots. I had no back-ups to stand by me in front of her Mom's rage.

Her look was so frenzied that it could make any other guy unconsciously squeeze out his bladder and wet his pants, but I was definitely different. I was scared but my love for her daughter sparked a new grit in me. After all, I was truly in love - *the kind of love which people call a love beyond words* - and I would do anything for it. Breaking the long pause, I mustered some courage to mumble out something to her.

"Aunt, please don't scold Tanya for anything. It was totally my fault. It was I who pressed her. I genuinely love…"

A hard tight slap on my right cheek completed my sentence. Her face went red; she was boiling in anger. Her anger could not abate my emotions. My eyes got wet, I didn't know whether it was the slap or it was the worry for Tanya that made me cry. But that moment, I just loved crying, it was the thing which I needed the most that instant.

"How dare you touch my daughter? How dare you?" She screamed.

"I am sorry; please don't punish Tanya for this!" I groaned as I feared what she could do to Tanya with this intense anger.

"Get out now otherwise I will call the police!" She screamed and her voice chocked as she burst into tears.

"Please don't cry!" I tried to be as gentle as possible. My gentleness had a reward - the hardest slap of my life - on my left cheek.

"Will you just leave?" She yelled in her tear-clogged voice, directing me towards the main gate.

21
Alvida

Her anger brought enormous rage in my eyes. I didn't say a word but I didn't like what she did at all. The colour of my cheeks that time could easily tell that I had been thrashed, harder on the left one. I lowered my eyes, took my bag and moved ahead towards the gate. I was angry, not because she slapped me but because she could not even understand that I really loved her daughter.

Before exiting the main gate of Tanya's house, I stopped and looked back at the garage, to have that *one-last-glimpse* of the venue of my most memorable intimate moment, but the sight that I saw touched even my angry soul - Tanya's mom was sitting and crying with her head in her hands. The headlights of the car were still on giving a vivid picture of her remorse. It seemed as if she was the protagonist of some sentimental drama with headlights of the car working as spot-lights. *(Oh, I love being mean when I am angry!)*

While observing the scene, I noticed something of my concern, lying on the greasy ground of the garage, just in front of her feet. Instantly, I rushed back to the garage only to make her more pissed off. Before she could fire anything at me, I bent in front of her feet.

She thought that I was going to touch her feet and therefore she moved two steps backwards. Interestingly, her moan was stopped with my bizarre action and only my beloved's cry was audible providing a faint *emotional-as-well-as-melodious* background music.

She might have been disappointed to notice that - *'for me, there was something more important than her feet.'* I picked up the souvenir of my first date - Tanya's left-over ice-cream cone from the ground. It still contained some drops of ice-cream left in it, though they were somewhat mixed with dust. My first date turned out to be my last date. It was worth collecting the memento of my first date to soothe my broken heart.

Before she threw me out of her home or gave me another threat of *calling the police*, I rushed to the main gate and made the swiftest-exit possible. Tanya's wailing faded as I trudged ahead. That fading sound could never fade away from my memory and it continued to restrain me from falling asleep for almost whole of a month to come.

I missed Tanya's presence by my side. I was all alone with just some dogs following me on the road. I carefully looked at the half-cone in the vague light and adored its texture. It had the fragrance of Tanya in it. I didn't know what was ahead, how things were going to turn out, the only thing I could do was to pray that Tanya's mom did not shower her rage upon her.

I moved ahead and crossed the same ice-cream booth, which screwed-up my condition by making me realize that I was bankrupt - with not even a single penny in my pocket.

I had no money to help me reach the nearest metro station or the auto stand, nor could I be so sure of finding a nice auto-driver who would trade my stuff with him. My stuff at that time included just a simple ball-point pen, handkerchiefs, a Prakriti-inhibiting tablet, a half used bottle of Axe and not to forget my souvenir – *which was priceless for me as well as for everyone else* - in different respects, though.

Mistiming and foul play had snatched the opportunity to even borrow money from Tanya. I recalled how my day started - a kick-ass kick-off bestowed by my mom and then Tanya's mom giving it a perfect finish by literally kicking my ass. It seemed as if all this was deliberately crafted by *the Master Craftsman* - everything being strategically planned in His daily planner.

Trotting ahead, I reached the corner of the road - the same corner where I had waited for her call two hours ago. Flood of memories crept in and they brought sudden tears to my eyes. I wanted to cry - cry my heart out to shed all my despair. I moved ahead with just a dim hope in my mind that everything would be normal in a few days. The word *'days'* was just to comfort my mind, I inwardly knew that it might turn out to be a month or a year or NEVER.

Still, I had hope and that was what kept me normal. I forged ahead and left her locality far behind, but my heart could not get far from her. It was longing for her as never before. The longing increased with every step I took. I was in despair, just wishing that all these happenings were just an illusion.

I pinched my skin to test if the whole thing was mere an illusion, but taking away the last shred of hope from me, it turned out to hurt me. I had unconscious tears flowing out of my eyes slowly as I walked, I wasn't crying though.

8.50 pm. I moved ahead realizing that there were no ways possible for me to be able to return to my hostel that day. *'I could hire an auto straight to my hostel and pay him then and there only by taking the money from my room'*, Came the idea but it could not turn fruitful.

My hostel was about two and half hours from Tanya's place and there was not a single auto-wala ready to undertake that long journey despite being offered with lots of money. The unavailability of the passengers on the return journey from my place was the chief reason. Tasting defeat all the way, I forged ahead.

The metro linkage connecting the north and south Delhi made the road transport from these two portions of the city less frequent - especially at night. The frequency of autos and buses in these routes are less, and at night there are almost no modes of transport available other than the metro.

I trod ahead and started feeling tired and sleepy at the same time. The adventure all through the day drained off energy from each and every cell of my body. All I wanted to do was to have a place to sit and relax. My mind needed more rest than my body since it had experienced more ups and downs all through the day.

9.10 pm. I walked at my painfully slow speed for another twenty minutes with my mind revolving around every thing that happened throughout my special day. Finally, I reached the same dilapidated bus-stop where Tanya and I had stopped and did *something*.

Being totally convinced that I would not be able to get back to my hostel, I SMSed Aryan that I had an urgent work to do and so I would not attend classes the next day.

He replied, "Oh yeah! I know what work you have! Don't forget to take precautions buddy!"

Even Aryan got to know that I was on a date. I knew what they must be thinking. They were considering me an even bigger stud, after-all in their views I managed a one night stand on my first date itself. *Dirty minds, they are!*

Giving alms to my body begging for rest, I sat down on the step at the bus-stop thinking about Tanya all the while. Sleep started diffusing my eyes so I took my bag down and cautiously placed the souvenir in it. I came across the Prakriti-inhibiting tablet in the bag and I consciously swallowed it even without water. I had no choice; I had to curtail Prakriti from calling me in that tough time. I put the bag on my side and sat on its straps, in a way securing it. I unfastened my wrist watch and put it into my pocket and prepared to have a doze.

I put my head down on my knees and in a few minutes, I went to sleep. Despite the sound of the engines and horns thumping my ears all through the night, I had a very deep sleep - probably due to the weariness I had fallen into, or perhaps my mind wanted to run away from everything that happened that day. It was surprisingly early time for me to sleep because in my hostel, a person would be considered abnormal if he slept before 1 o' clock at night.

I was having a doze. I had a dream – a dream of Tanya and me together and it soothed all my sufferings. But, dreams seldom turn into reality. I did not want to get up from that beautiful trance to the tougher realities. I slept unconcerned about the world and the pains which it had inflicted on me the day before.

Part 4

Pyaar ke Side-Effects

22
The Difficult Days

I opened my eyes to find myself on the same stair where I had parked my cold butt the day before. I got up and stretched. I could feel myself quite energized after such a refreshing sleep. However, my nose was blocked; Delhi's cold-summer night took its price.

I took out my watch to notice the time. It was 6.15 am and the date was 28th July - officially, the first day of the new semester. My friends might have got up enthusiastically and were getting ready for their classes. The first class of the semester sees the maximum attendance of all time with the torture-theatres being jam-packed with *home-food-nourished-fleshy-buttocks* – their number being twice the number of seats.

I, unfortunately, was going to miss all my classes even though I had got up on time, rather before time. I took out my mobile to see if there were any missed calls only to find that my mobile too had got discharged over the night

My nose was struggling hard to breathe. Trying its level best to clear the blockages, in the process it forced me to employ my handkerchief. I looked at the ground for my bag, but I could not find it anywhere at the bus-stop. After a lot of searching, I did find my sweaty handkerchief thrown on the muddy ground on the road. In a split second, I was enlightened - my bag had been stolen while I was sleeping. My rumps did not offer much friction to stop the straps of the bag being dragged from beneath my bottom.

I was laughing at the poor luck of the thief, who would have received as his prize two used-handkerchiefs – of which he threw the sweaty one on the road, a five-buck pen and an almost-empty bottle of deodorant resting peacefully in that withered bag. The bag was also too old for inflicting pain of loss in my heart. Suddenly something struck me that wiped out my laugh in a second - *my souvenir was also in that bag*. The feeling of losing the memento of my beloved made me go mad. I did not care about the other contents of the bag; just losing that half-cone brought immense distress to me. I searched all over the bus-stop for the thing, but my eyes failed to focus even a simple shape like a half-cone on the retina. Upset, I went back to the same place to sit in disappointment and lowered my face with disgust.

My eyes were looking at the reflection of the sun on the road. I began moving my eyes to and fro, much like a pendulum. My vision reached beside my leg, and lo, there was a surprise waiting for me.

I could see the cone thrown down on the ground right next to my right feet. A stream of joy and relief made me jump on the road. The thief or the beggar, whosoever, might have checked my stuff and after finding the valueless cone, he would have angrily thrown it at me. What else could he expect from a person who used a bus-stand like his bedroom? He made my day since the half-cone which was valueless for him, was *invaluable* for me.

I caught hold of the cone and smelled it. It had lost its aroma. But, it could not make my mind lose the memory of Tanya's fragrance. It acted as a trigger provoking Tanya's fragrance every time I smelled it.

Happy at last, I looked up and observed the baby sun slowly rising in the sky. The sun's funny light tickled my body and brought a feeling of warmth. I realized that my blocked nose was automatically cleared in the hurried hunt for the souvenir. For the first time in my life had I got up so early on my own - *without even any bhow-bhow*.

Appreciating the beauty of nature – *the so called Prakriti* – at dawn made me feel really rejuvenated.

I channeled my feelings to Him, "So, You have done some constructive work as well! You happen to be multi-talented! Good Yaar!"

I looked at my wrist watch once again and observed the date carefully. It was 28th July, which meant that 'my special day' – the day I had visualized in my dreams for more than a thousand times had passed. 27th July had become a past memory and that too an unforgettable past, thanks to His innumerable arts and crafts in beautifying it.

My third semester had started, bringing the most interesting dawn of my lifetime. I was there with no money, no battery in my cell and no ideas of what I was going to do.

I had faced enough of misery, and there were more to come. But considering this novel, it's a love story. And a love story can't go on and on with just a single character, no matter how brilliant (*like me!*) he may be. As goes the saying, behind every successful man, there is a woman, I concluded that – *behind every unsuccessful man there is a rusted-iron-pillar of a bus-stand.*

So I don't want to deal about how I reached back to my hostel since it would include about a dozen more instances - which means a dozen more interesting chapters like '*The Ambulance lift*', '*The Shopper's Stop*', and '*The Unforgettable Bus Ride*'. But sure, I can tell you how my love story took its twists and turns and went ahead.

On 28th July, I managed to reach my hostel at about 2 pm in the afternoon, after yet another series of moments of 'Oops', making it another saga of adventure. Reaching the hostel, the first thing I did was that - I placed the souvenir inside my cupboard securing it forever since it was my most personal possession.

The next thing that I did was that I closed my door and cried my head off on my bed. Almost the whole of my pillow was drenched with my tears as well as sweat - *the summer of Delhi can even dry your tears!*

My return journey ordeal had made me exhausted enough to push my body to seek rest. I wanted to sleep, but I just could not sleep no matter how hard I tried, the pangs of separation from Tanya were killing me from inside.

28th July

5 pm. The students – who are better known as the cream of the nation – returned to the hostel. Instead of landing into their rooms, they were in my room. It looked as if all of them had forgotten the way to their rooms. There I lay on my bed, the tear-factory of my eyes momentary enjoying a tea-break, with all the thirty five batch-mates of my hostel blessing me with their divine presence. My room was having the privilege to have more cream than a cup of vanilla itself. I could not get what the special occasion was that demanded their creamy presence. Aryan and Anuj led the whole gang. Interestingly, Sameer was not there.

"Hi!" I stammered. My eyes had a tough time facing seventy eyes at the same time. My 'Hi' was more of a public speaking for me. I got up and opened the window to let *air-with-the-mosquitoes* enter the suffocating place.

"Hiiiiii Kanaaaaav!" They said in chorus, voices in harmonics. Their incisors began to show, majority of them being off-white in color. Cigarettes and erratic water supply for the *one-pm-bed-risers* were the unrecognized artists behind that coloring/discoloring.

"How was the night?" Anuj asked. I could hear some laughs coming from the people far-off, hidden from my 5'9" vision.

"And also the day?" Aryan added his parenthesis to the previous statement.

I realized where their intention was targeted at. For the *majority-nerdy-crowd* of IIT, a *night-stand* during college life is no less an achievement than winning a Nobel Prize for Physics or Chemistry, the former being much more difficult in fact. They were curious and also a bit envious, after all. But this curiosity could not prevent my temper from rising high.

"Yeah, I did not know you had so much stamina! You played for twenty four hours man! It calls for a *toast.*" Anuj continued.

If I was given a hunter, I would play with them for more than hundred hours!

The mum spectators around had occasional gags marking the end of every sentence spoken. I could see even some of the ultra-geeks in the crowd. They were having their first-time recreation out of their room besides their library and computer labs. *Yeah, library and labs count in their recreation.*

"I will have vodka!" Aryan said even though nobody asked for that scoundrel's opinion. I could feel that the mastermind behind that special gathering was Aryan.

I was just one step short of bombardment. Aryan's next statement provoked it in a single go.

"By the way, how was your Tanya – 'in bed'?" Aryan said. My temper knew no bounds. The anger against Aryan, his fellow-mates and the sorrow of the previous day made a ruthless potpourri.

"Go, have your vodka with your own shit. Bloody fuckers! Get out now! Bastards!" I erupted with my face bubbling in heat. It was the first time in my life I used these filthy words. They clearly understood that I was angry to a limit.

The whole cream of the nation was centrifuged in my single statement. No words or laughs could sputter out of their mouths. They had never seen me so furious before. The off-white incisors were neatly covered by lips – some even with moustaches. Silently, they retraced their steps back and found the way back to their respective rooms.

23 The Hopeful Romantic

28th July – 3rd Aug

You might be wondering what happened to Tanya. I did not dare to call her for the next two days. However, on the third day i.e. 30th July, I called her mobile when the reply was, *"The number you are trying to reach is not in service"*.

I realized that her mom had her grounded and she might have discarded her sim card. I did not dare to call on her land-line since I knew she would never be allowed to receive the phone - it would be her mother or some maid.

Over the last three days of the month though, I became very desperate - missing her more than ever.

1st Aug

I gathered some courage and called at her landline from a PCO. The first time her mother picked up the phone. Nervous, I disconnected the phone instantly. I called again an hour later, only to find her mom again at the landline. It seemed she was affixed with fevicol on the phone itself. I again disconnected.

The disappointment was not enough to lower my spirit. I persisted. Half an hour later, I called again, this time fully prepared on how to tackle any difficult situation. My ears got what it expected – again, it was Tanya's mom on the other side of the phone. I mimicked a girl and asked, "Hello aunty, is Tanya home? I am her friend Shreya."

"Tanya is not at home, she is out of station."

Confused, I could not digest what she just said.

Lost in thoughts and curiosity, I spoke up, "Where has she gone?" in my original voice.

These are the times when you want to strangle yourself with the electrified barbed-wires along the Line of Control(LOC), without even publishing your book.

I neither got the time to pursue what I wanted nor the time to repent on the blunder I committed since she exploded at me without making any delay.

"That's none of your concerns, Kanav!"

And then came the much-awaited bombardment targeted with all the evil-forces at *me*.

"How dare you call at my home? Didn't you get my warning the last time? I will lodge a police complaint against you and this time I am damn serious."

That meant that the last time she wasn't serious. I knew that even this time she wasn't serious, because my dear Tanya would tell her nothing about me.

"Where is Tanya? Is she all-right?" I persisted without getting moved by her warnings.

"You rascal! Stay away from my daughter! Now you see what I will do to you. Just wait and watch..." She disconnected the phone.

Her last words echoed in my ears for nearly half an hour. I was not afraid of the police thing, but I was definitely worried about what this ruthless mother could do to her daughter. Nevertheless, I did not dare to call at her place ever again!

Perplexed, I stood in the PCO, even after the phone was disconnected, wondering how I could get to know where Tanya actually was.

I had no choice other than being optimistic. I desperately expected that Tanya would call me sooner or later. I didn't want to imagine her situation at home, since that would make me more pessimistic. My expectations increased as the days passed. The expectation was so much that every time my phone rang with an unknown number, I would jump in excitement hoping that it was her call. My condition became much like the time after I had first met her.

I had to bear all these things on my own. I did not share what happened to me with anybody, not even my closest friends, fearing that they would make fun of me. Also, I liked to keep my personal life a bit aloof from my friends.

3rd Aug

A week passed, with me having no trace of where Tanya was. Finding myself quite insufficient to dig out any information of Tanya, I called our common friend Ruchi. I related to her everything that had happened *(excluding that brace scene!)* and asked her if she knew Tanya's whereabouts. Her answer startled me.

"Ok, now I realize what the real picture is!" She said.

"What do you mean?" I asked.

"Three days ago, she called me for just a minute saying that she would not be coming to college for a few days as she is going to her maternal uncle's place. She did not tell me the reason why she was going but I could make out from her voice that something was wrong because the badminton championship was on and she had missed all of them"

"Where exactly is her maternal uncle's place? Any idea?" I asked.

"No idea, she never mentioned about it earlier. Nor could I ask her that day when she called last time because she disconnected the call in just a minute." Ruchi said.

"I just wonder how she is. Can you just go to her place when you get time and check it out whenever you get time?" I requested genuinely.

"I too am equally worried. I will go to her place in a day or so and check her whereabouts. I will inform you as soon as I get any information. Don't worry!" She assured me.

Ruchi began her statement saying she is equally worried and she ended it with a 'Don't worry!' *Strangely complicated!*

"Thanks a ton. I will be waiting for your call. B'bye!" I said as I disconnected the phone.

The next two days I waited for Ruchi's call more than anything else. I had not waited for anybody's call so desperately, *not even Tanya's call*, as I waited for her call that day. My whole life revolved around her single call. I could literally feel the time; each and every tick of my wrist-watch resonated with my heartbeat.

I realized what Tanya's condition must have been. She had been grounded - no outings, no phone-calls and not even college. All these things were quite contrary to her character which was quite outgoing and exuberant. That's the living example of how strict a mother can be! *(I wanted to use the word demonic in place of strict, but considering she is my to-be-mother-in-law, I need to pay some respect!)*

All I prayed for everyday was Tanya's well being. I was turned into a theist from a hardcore atheist after I felt the pangs of separation between me and my love. I could not sleep that night thinking about Tanya all the while. Intuitively, I knew she too would be missing me like hell all these days.

I affixed a big poster in my room saying,

"Hope is all I have
You are all I need"

to help me never lose my unending hope.

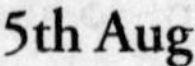

5th Aug

Ruchi didn't call me the other day; it took her almost two days to give me the proper information. I became desperate to know about Tanya and after not receiving Ruchi's call during the first half of the second day, I myself called Ruchi in the evening.

"Hey Ruchi, it's Kanav!"

"Hi Kanav."

"I was waiting for your call for the last two days. Why didn't you call? Did you get to meet Tanya?"

"I could not meet her. Yesterday I went twice to her place but it was locked..."

"Didn't you go to her place today?" I asked almost interrupting her statement mid way, my voice clearly giving a hint of annoyance.

"I didn't need to go to her place today. I met her mom today, she came to my college."

"What for? Isn't she satisfied with all the tortures she laid on Tanya that she needed to come to college?"

I presumed that she must have gone to see the college-counselor regarding Tanya. Still, I was not happy as the matter got very serious. Her mom indeed was very stern. *I would be having a tough time in the future, I laughed at the thought.*

"I could not muster up the courage to tell you the matter which took place today." She explained.

"What happened Ruchi? Is Tanya all-right?" I was tense, intuitively knowing that something unpleasant was going to strike my ears.

"I could not meet Tanya, but today in the college, her mom came to get her Transfer Certificate. I went forward to greet her and ask about

Tanya's whereabouts only to get to know that Tanya has left the country on 2nd Aug for the United States to her maternal uncle's place."

Frozen to death, my mind went crazy. I experienced an earthquake without an earthquake. I just could not believe what I had just heard. I was dumbstruck, with my mind completely blank. Ruchi continued while I tried to regain myself…

"I asked her why Tanya did not even tell me about it. She dismissed it saying that it was a family matter and was very urgent. She ended her conversation with 'Sorry, I am in a hurry. I will ask Tanya to call you'." Ruchi said.

"Is that all?" I asked with my voice clearly giving a hint of my shock.

"I am very sorry Kanav. I can understand how you feel…" She sympathized.

"Bye." I said without even hearing her sympathy and disconnected the phone.

No matter what she said, she could not understand how I felt because if she could, then she would definitely have got a nervous breakdown.

5th Aug - 9th Aug

I did not eat anything for the next two days after Ruchi's last call. I had never been so frenzied earlier; all my love was shattered in a moment. It could not have happened – Tanya running away from me – without leaving any trace of her. I felt like killing myself for being the cause of never-ending sorrow to me as well as Tanya.

I restricted myself inside the walls of my room. I liked my virtual cage. Everyday, while going for classes I would see numerous smiling faces, all of them making me jealous. My happiness was away from me

– distant and lost. I was lonely without Tanya; she was all I had in life. I could not even imagine myself without her. My whole world revolved around her and suddenly *my world* had moved to the other side of this globe. It was not fair; God had played a big gamble with me, with loss and only loss on my side.

I started keeping aloof from my hostel friends and preferred seclusion. Even my friends became a bit aloof from me considering how badly I had rebuked them when the gang attacked my room. I wanted to ease my pain on my own and had a tough time.

I got no further news of Tanya and day by day my hope diminished. I surrendered to fate. Metaphorically, my fate was much like a robot for me, with its remote control in her mom's hands.

The *hopeful romantic* had become less expectant and more pessimistic. I had no complains with Tanya considering she might be having a difficult time trying to find ways to contact me from the US. I tried to provide my mind with a valid reason to explain for her not being able to contact me. The most probable reason seemed that it might be possible that her maternal uncle - *with the same genes as her mother* - would be far more rigid and strict.

Every morning I got up with an iota of hope and switched on my laptop to check my mails only to find out spams and forwards from the same old friends. I mailed Tanya everyday describing what I had done the whole day, how much I loved her and how much I was missing her. Then I would sign in her account and reply back to the mails I sent to her – telling how much she loved me and was missing me, giving my sad mind a sympathizing treatment.

The disappointment of receiving no information at all, through any source whatsoever, that I faced every morning performed the latent work of killing my hope on a daily basis. Nights would be restless and no matter whatever I tried I could not sleep. I started using tranquilizers to fight my insomnia and my condition worsened day by day. Almost all my hostel-mates began regarding me as a psycho drug-addict and maintained a safe distance from me.

For about the next two weeks, I came back to my room everyday after my classes and used to lock it from inside just to sit in front of Tanya's photos in remembrance. I relived all those little moments of fun we had together, all those intimacies, all those teasing, cat-fights and cuddlings. The more I recalled each of those moments, the lonelier I would become.

Though my mind had apparently surrendered, my heart was still waiting for her to come back. I took out the souvenir from my cupboard and kept it on my table forever to let her never become a memory to let her always be there by my side.

0th Aug. 1.30 am.

was sobbing, quite audibly at night. Someone knocked at my door. It ad been the first knock in the third semester. After my outburst that ay, no-one dared to even step in the vicinity of my room. I wiped my ce and opened the door.

"Are you crying Kanav? What's wrong? Share it with me." Sameer id.

"Leave me alone." I rebuked Sameer. This rebuke was not like the ormal joking rebukes that I offered to him. It was emotional. Tears arted rolling down.

"Hey yaar, what happened?" Sameer asked with concern and entered y room.

I related to him the whole of story. For the first time, he listened all throughout without saying even a word. I found a true friend in hin and related to him all my sorrows. It was the first time that I share my tragic story with any other person completely.

"You got an inspiration to work hard and make it to US. Very fev people get an internship to US after second year. Just put all you efforts for it."

I was perplexed. His angle of looking at thing was unique and fc the first time did I feel that he really had an ability to motivate.

"Cheer up! Remember only the good things. At least, you have nc lost her forever. Consider Anuj, do you know that Niti dumped him Sameer pacified.

"Really? But why?" I asked. Sameer's gossipy news made me curiou and helped forget my pain for a while.

"Anuj being a despo was never satisfied. He always thought that l could have got a better looking girl than Niti. And one day, Niti caug him red-handed hanging out with her own room-mate."

I laughed out. It was the first laugh in the past ten days.

"Isn't he upset?" I asked.

"Oh Anuj. You know how Anuj is! He is busy finding his next Nik on Orkut."

Around 15-20 Aug

The next few days, Sameer made it a point to accompany my up self. His company soothed my pain and he had an innate ability spark off interesting conversation about love, life and career. I surprisin found myself quite interested in the subject of *philosophy*.

"Why is Tanya not contacting me?" I asked Sameer one day. I v feeling irritated, once again.

"Stop fretting around. She must be having a tough time there

America. Let me change the topic, otherwise you would keep niggling. Ok, wait...umm…what should I ask? Yeah, tell me how you proposed to her the first time." Sameer asked and tried to divert my mind to good things.

I related to him the Barista incident. He was fascinated by that idea of the "Scrabble proposal".

"Did you think that on your own?" Sameer asked.

"Yeah. Love makes you creative, you know!" I said.

"Awesome man. I am going to try that out soon." Sameer said.

"Soon? You like someone?" I asked.

"Kind of." He blushed.

"Who? Who's that?" I poked him. My curiosity knew no bounds.

"Reva! Strike a bell?" He said and his cheek reddened.

"Oh Reva! Bloody fatty! You too – an underdog? By the way, you know what? You two suit each other. Both of you are chatter-boxes, after-all. But how did you befriend her after that mall-incident?"

"Remember last semester. You used to lock your room from inside and I was left alone. I thereafter began chatting with her over net and then shifted over phone. I can see something is cropping up between us." He chuckled.

Sameer's statement surprised me. I could never expect that he too could develop a liking for somebody and that too Reva, oh my God! Nevertheless, he turned out to be the most matured of all of us. His standing by my side helped me gather myself.

Around 24-25th Aug

As time passed, it soothed my pangs of separation. Sameer replaced the monotony of my life and brought all the four friends together. Time flew at an astounding pace and the hectic class schedule could not make me realize that almost one month had passed since my *special day.*

I had got no news of Tanya in the past twenty days and my optimism had been buried due to the insurmountable academic pressure of my institute. The classes used to leave me tired at the end of the day, and as a result Tanya stopped disturbing me at night. My tranquilizer-stricken persona was restored back to its normal state. But, the effervescence of my character was lost somewhere in the sands of time.

Aryan and Anuj had their own lives which were quite rugged and therefore didn't bother me with sarcasm. Sameer brought joy to me every once in a while when I felt low and helped me become social again. I became gregarious consciously - much like my hostel-mates - to engage my idle mind somewhere. Their company did make a difference in my attitude, but it could not provide anything for my aching heart. I tried to become much like how I was in the first year – a withdrawn guy yet ready to take part in all the mischief.

Inwardly, I still longed for Tanya! Her missing presence left an irreparable wound in my heart. Four days later, my birthday was coming and I was not at all excited about it.

24
The End

29th Aug

12 am. My birthday arrived. It was my 19th birthday. The last teen year was now on and it made me feel as if I had started aging. Time had moved on quite fast and I was standing there cutting my birthday cake with my friends. Friends sang 'Happy birthday' in their unique tunes making a good remix of the original version.

Just after I cut my cake, my face became innately decorated with the cake, leaving no part of my face exposed to the environment. After that, my butt got warmed up severely with about a hundred birthday bumps. My friends made sure that my bottom got so much roasted that I would not be able to sit in the morning classes.

Calls, calls and calls. Calls from friends – the old, forgotten ones; calls from relatives – distant as well as close and calls from my parents made me feel that the day was indeed 'My Day'. Still, my heart's vague longing for the one special call did not get fulfilled.

Ruchi called to wish me birthday and made me recall the about bet that I'd lost in her last birthday. She fixed a meeting the next day, since she was conscious that I was sad inwardly, and wanted to cheer me up. A bit contented at the sudden importance I was seeking from everybody around, I just wandered around with my phone buzzing all throughout.

I went back to my friends' company, who were having a great time relishing yummy pizzas, cold drinks and cake. I had provided them with a good respite from the morbid hostel food and they too conferred on me a magnanimous gift called BUMPS – hundreds of them!

But, friends are friends. They are the ones who make you happy and indeed I was somewhat happy.

Yeah, I was happy! Happy, but not quite elated. Amidst all my closest friends who were present, I missed the presence of *somebody* – '*my-bestest-friend*'. I was not really enjoying the on-going birthday bash. Though I affixed a plastic smile on my face, I wanted some solitude.

After having a slice of the cake, I sneaked back to my room. My friends thought that I was going to wash my face and therefore they didn't question where I was heading to!

I entered my room and looked into the mirror. My face was so well decorated that I could not even realize that it was me. It seemed as if I had a facial of vanilla, chocolate and cherries. I washed my face and came back to my room looking somewhat '*Chikna*'.

I switched off the lights and lay down on my bed thinking about that *somebody*. Minutes later, I switched on the table-lamp and held Tanya's photo and the souvenir in my hands. Seeing her innocuous smile, I hammered in my mind that *no distance can reduce my love for her.* I sat on my chair with the half-cone in my hand with the light of the table-lamp making a silhouette of the cone in the background. I was missing her - as never before.

As time passed, I started getting more emotional. Seeing that this phase would continue to grow as time passed, I decided to cheer up my mood. I got up from the chair and switched the lights on. I shrugged and switched on my laptop to play hard-rock music at the highest volume. With my laptop on in front of me, I found it a good time to check my mails, notifications and scraps on the internet - after all, it was my birthday.

12:45 am. I signed into my Orkut account with my id - *kanav.bajaj* and password - *alldayidreamabouttanya* just to notice that there was an increment in my scraps by almost a century.

Scrolling down the scrapbook, all I could see was my so-called miser acquaintance friends wishing me *'Happy Birthday'* in seemingly festive mood. Their fakeness was clearly visible, as some of them wrote - '*I want a treat*'. They did not even bother to call me to wish and now they were demanding a treat. Extremely pissed off, I didn't even reply a *'Thank you'* to any of them.

Nevertheless, in order to prioritize my acquaintances in a hierarchical order, I flipped through the pages of the scrapbook to get to know who amongst them was the first person to wish me a 'Happy Birthday'.

Interestingly, the first scrap was from an unknown person with no profile picture and '.....' as its name. It said - *'Happy Birthday. May God give you everything you wish.'*

Bursting with curiosity, I instantly clicked on the profile link. The slow internet speed of my hostel took its own time to open the webpage and played with my curiosity like hell. The profile opened after taking two long painstaking minutes and this was what I saw as the *about me* -

"I look up at the velvety blackness of the sky
And I see stars adorning nights dress so bright
Even diamonds may feel shy

And then I see one
That breaks free and shoots to
I know not where
Oh little star!
Will you take my wish to him who is so far
Tell him that I am
Just a little lonely here...

Hi jerk,
Wanna play Scrabble?"

P.S. This was just the beginning...

Epilogue

Hi…

I am back. Don't I sound happy? Things are finally falling into place for me as well as for my friends.

After scores of break-ups and patch-ups, Aryan and Riya are still together. Indeed, Riya turned out to be Aryan's *third* lucky charm. Aryan is gay and contented.

Having crashed through Neetika, Nikita and Niti, Anuj's girl-hunt is currently paused at somebody named Niki. Nevertheless, his search for somebody better is still on, whenever he gets a chance.

Sameer went on an informal date with Reva. Following my footsteps, he laid down the letters L,I,E,V,U,O,Y,O on the board but received an "EVILYOU" back. Puzzled, he put a TOO after it and said the same. They did not share a word after that. He is having a tough time choosing between suicide and murder.

Tanya was definitely having a tough time there in US. Her maternal uncle was very strict – much more than what I had presumed. But, she still managed to give me that perfect surprise on my birthday.

Coming back to me, I am working hard and my grades have significantly improved. Love indeed proved to be an inspiration for me. I have got an internship in US for two months during the summer of the coming year. I hope I would be able to make up for the last one year of loneliness in those two months.

Tanya's semester will end by January. She is coming to India in Feb and will be here on Ruchi's birthday. We persuaded Ruchi to keep the venue of her next birthday to be the same restaurant 'Waikiki'. I am ready to get dazzled by Tanya's scintillating presence, once again.

And what else, even my enemy God became my friend; I can now say that I've a divine friend.

So finally, the thing *that I couldn't even have imagined in my dreams* has materialized here in my own hands. And as I said, this is just the beginning…